BOY
of the BORDER

By Arna Bontemps and Langston Hughes

Illustrated by Antonio Castro L.

BOY
of the BORDER

By Arna Bontemps and Langston Hughes

Illustrated by Antonio Castro L.

SWEET EARTH FLYING PRESS

Published by Sweet Earth Flying Press LLC
508 Tawny Oaks Place
El Paso, Texas 79912

Boy of the Border is published courtesy of the James Weldon Johnson Memorial Collection, Yale Collection of American Literature, Beinecke Rare Book and Manuscript Library

Book jacket and book design by
Antonio Castro Graphic Design Studio

Many thanks to Sculptor Gregory Elliott for the beautiful handcarved piece of leather used for the cover of this book.

Library of Congress Control Number: 2008930191

ISBN: 978-0-9790987-0-3

Printed in the United States of America
Manufactured by Thomson-Shore, Dexter MI (USA) #555MS525
November 2009

Contents

I.   The Bronco Herd .... · 5

II.   Bandits .... · 13

III.   A Story Beneath the Stars .... · 25

IV.   Cactus Country .... · 35

V.   A River Crossing .... · 41

VI.   Bow and Arrow .... · 51

VII.   So Far To Go .... · 65

VIII. The New Colt .... · 69

IX.   Sandstorm .... · 75

X.   Journey's End .... · 83

XI.   City of the Angels .... · 91

XII.   And Back Again .... · 97

Afterword .... · 107

Chapter I

The Bronco Herd

Miguel woke up suddenly. The shutters were still drawn in the little bedroom where he slept, but there was a great commotion outside. A clatter of trampling hoofs rose from the street. Above this noise, the boy could hear the shouts of hard-voiced men. Miguel jumped from his bed, hurriedly ran to the window and flung the shutters wide. Nothing could be seen but a cloud of dust. A moment later somebody was pounding on the gate and jangling the bell. Miguel began putting on his clothes.

Miguel was a slender, brown boy with hair that always fell in his eyes. He lived in a sturdy little house with a patio and a surrounding wall in the northern part of Mexico. But he was not alone in that house, and as he dressed he wondered if his father or mother, his little sister, the cook, or the cook's tall son who worked in the yard, had heard the noise in the street, the pounding at the gate, or the jangling of the bell. Miguel finished buttoning his clothes and ran to the front door. For a moment, the bright early morning sunshine dazzled him.

By that time, Maximiliano, the yard boy, was shouting to someone over the gate and Señor Del Monte, Miguel's father, was hurrying through the patio to find out who it was. A moment later Miguel saw that there was nothing to be disturbed about. Everybody commenced to laugh heartily together as a big man in a white sombrero came through the gate and shook hands with Señor Del Monte.

"Mario!" exclaimed Señor Del Monte, greeting his brother-in-law. "What a surprise!"

A powerfully built man was Miguel's Uncle Mario. His hair was long and as shiny as a crow's feathers. He had a heavy mustache. On one finger he wore a large silver ring shaped like the head of a wolf. It had two small rubies for eyes. There were silver spurs on his riding boots. He smiled broadly as Miguel came through the patio to join the others.

"Ah, there's the fellow I've come to get," he laughed, throwing out his arms to his young nephew. "How about it, Miguel? I'll need lots of hands on this long trip. You are coming with me?"

Of course, Miguel couldn't answer. He'd lost his breath. But his father spoke up for him.

"What are you up to, Mario?" he asked with a twinkle. "First you scare us out of our wits with all this noise. Now you talk about a trip. What's up your sleeve?"

Uncle Mario laughed loudly, throwing back his head with good humor.

"I surprised you, did I? Well, you can never tell about Uncle Mario," he said. "If I had a fine family like yours, Elegio, I might be different, but a bachelor like me sometimes gets restless sitting at his fireplace all the time. The fact is this, I wasn't satisfied with the price the buyers were offering for three-year-old broncos this year. Fine young colts and fillies are worth more than just eight or ten pesos a head, and I told them so in right strong language. To tell the truth, I ran them off my ranch when they talked like that."

"I'll bet you didn't bite your tongue, Mario," Miguel's father smiled. "but what's that got to do with this trip you talk about and that monstrous herd trampling outside the wall there?"

"I'm taking some of my young horses up to the border and across. I want to see what I can get for them in the States, Elegio."

"Across the border!"

"Yep, and a good ways across, too. I'm thinking about Los Angeles."

Miguel's heart skipped two or three beats. All the way from northern Mexico to Los Angeles with a herd of wild horses! California! It seemed impossible.

"Why, that's where Aunt Chona lives," Miguel said, still unbelieving.

"You're right, Miguel," his uncle answered. "Chona lives there, and that's part of the reason I'm going. She's told me lots of times in her letters that they sell unbroken broncos there in the plaza for ten dollars a head. Sometimes more. That's what I'm counting on. I've got about three hundred horses with me."

Señor Del Monte shook his head as if he were puzzled.

"We can count on you to think up odd things, Mario," he said. "but come on inside now. Breakfast will be ready by the time you get that dust off you."

"Breakfast—ah, that's the word. But I can't let my horsemen keep the road cluttered up while I eat."

"Maximiliano will lead them to the fields," Miguel's father said, pointing. "A little later we'll have the cook send your men something to eat."

The two men went through the patio and entered the house. Miguel followed Maximiliano to the gate and watched the yardboy as he directed the horsemen to the field his father had indicated. The wild young broncos were not behaving any too well. They bit each other, kicked up their heels, tried to break away from the rest of the herd, and in general displayed their wild ways and bad manners. Yet they were a beautiful lot with long, full tails and flowing manes, gleaming in the sun. Looking at them, it was hard for Miguel to imagine that they were all as untamed as jackrabbits. Not one of the herd had ever known a saddle or a bridle or a corral. But a horse is a magnificent animal, even when he's wild, and Miguel loved these just as he loved all horses.

The yardboy returned, opened the big double gates, and brought Uncle Mario's own horse with an extra one around to the corral in the yard. Miguel closed the gates.

After breakfast Uncle Mario went out to his men and made sure they were all right. He returned smiling and announced that he had not only gained a nearby peasant's permission for the young horses to remain in the field all day, but had also arranged for the horsemen to take turns sleeping in a tiny adobe house nearby. This was a relief to Uncle Mario, for now he could enjoy the rest of the day visiting with his relatives.

Señor Del Monte, who had said nothing for a long time, put on a smock and began mixing paints. He was an artist and was in the habit of painting in the patio everyday. When he had visitors, like today, he went right ahead with his pictures and entertained them as he worked. The rest of the family made themselves comfortable on the outdoor chairs.

"Los Angeles," he said suddenly, as if he had never ceased to think about Uncle Mario's plan. "You're really set on it, hunh?"

"Set on it? Why, I'm already on my way. The border is no more than a hundred miles from here. Then the real trip will begin—across the Arizona desert to Los Angeles."

"I wonder if you haven't forgotten something in planning this trip, Mario," Miguel's mother asked.

"Forgotten something? What?"

"Hasn't Antonio written to you?"

Antonio was Miguel's big seventeen-year-old brother. He had gone down to Mexico City to study art. He had been gone only a month or two, but he had written back to say that the train which carried him southward had been fired on by bandits. Some of the windows were broken out and passengers had to lie on the floor to keep from being shot. There had been a revolution in Mexico and parts of the country were very unsettled.

"Bandits?" Uncle Mario asked his sister.

"They are raiding villages and stealing horses up this way now. Wouldn't they enjoy coming across a herd like yours on the plains?"

"Let them try it," Uncle Mario said, setting his jaw firmly. "There aren't many of us, just three men besides me, but we won't take any bullying."

"Yet you want to take Miguel along with you?" the mother said.

Uncle Mario's eyes lost their sternness.

"Oh, Anna," he said, "your Antonio is a real man at seventeen. He saved a man's life when he was no more than fifteen by killing a black cougar just as the animal was about to pounce on the poor fellow. He's a man, but it looks like you're trying to make a candy man out of this little one."

"Of course I'm going, Uncle Mario," Miguel said, speaking up quickly. "Mama's going to let me. You see if she doesn't."

Señor Del Monte squeezed some more paint from a tube.

"The boy knows his mother," he smiled.

"Oh! I don't see how on earth I can do it," the mother sighed. "I agree with what you say, Mario, and I know you'll look out for him, but I just couldn't sleep with Miguel away out in the desert at his age. He's only just twelve this week you know."

"Aw, let him go, Mama," little Angelita said quite surprisingly. "Please, he wants a long horse ride. He's tired of just riding round and round in the corral every night. Maximiliano said so."

"So that's what you've been doing?" the father said, turning suddenly. "I noticed a chicken with a broken leg yesterday."

Miguel was embarrassed, but he didn't try to hide his guilt.

"I didn't mean to do that," he said softly. "It was an accident, but I never get any good rides."

Uncle Mario laughed.

"No good rides, you say? Well, just wait till we get

started. You may wish you'd never seen a saddle before it's over."

"But I haven't said he could go, Mario," the mother said almost tearfully, "not yet I haven't."

By now Miguel was overjoyed. He could tell by his mother's tone that she was about to say yes. And he could plainly see that his father would offer no objection. It was well-known that he did not want his sons to grow up soft. The mother, on the other hand, had complete confidence in her brother, and Miguel was used to seeing her yield to his persuasion.

"You may go, Miguel," she said.

Chapter II
Bandits
~∾∽~

The old folks sat on the patio and talked for
hours under the open sky, but Miguel went to bed early
and promptly fell asleep. The night was long because
he kept dreaming and waking up. Every time he closed
his eyes he saw something thrilling or dangerous or
beautiful. Once it was a hungry cougar showing his teeth
from a scrubby tree in a thicket. Again it was a horde
of bandits. They seemed to be in the corral behind the
house, terrifying the chickens and goats and leading the
family horses away. At still another time, it was a lovely
green spot that floated into his dream, a clump of trees
on a white desert. Miguel stretched his arms above his
head and rolled in his bed. When would tomorrow
come? It did not occur to him that it would be many,
many nights before he would sleep in a comfortable bed
like this again, nor did he care.

The day dawned finally, however, and Miguel got
up to find that his things had already been packed by
his mother and taken by Maximiliano to the provision
wagon in which they were to be carried. The sun was not
up high enough to shine over the mountains so the cook
had to put candles on the breakfast table. There were
two wicker platters piled high with buns of various sizes
and shapes, round, long, twisted, plain and sugared.
There was a crumbly white goat's cheese. And a bottle
of jet black very strong essence of coffee to be used
sparingly in enormous brown cups of hot milk poured
from an earthenware kettle that the cook kept on the
nearby charcoal grill.

By the time Miguel and Uncle Mario had finished, the herd was in the road outside the wall, ready to start on the journey accompanied by the rugged provision wagon. The goodbyes in the patio took a long time, as is always the case in countries like Mexico where families are very close together. There were many embraces, blessings, and not a few tears. This done, Uncle Mario got into his saddle, and Miguel, with some difficulty, got into the one provided for him. A moment later they were in the road, half lost in the dust kicked up by the horses, waving to the family and the servants who stood at the open gate with hands high as long as they could see anything at which to wave.

"That's Antonio's horse you're riding, Miguel," said Uncle Mario. "The one he always uses when he comes to my ranch."

"Gentle?"

"Oh, sure, very gentle."

"Fast too, I bet."

His uncle only smiled. Miguel's heart seemed to grow big in him. He was proud to be riding his older brother's horse, and he began to wonder if he would ever be as tall and brave as his brother. Then and there he made up his mind that he would not flinch at anything on this trip and above all things, he would not cry, not even once. If he felt timid or shaky, he would keep his feelings on the inside where they wouldn't show, like people did when they wished to hide a hole in the heel of a stocking. Maybe in that way he would get a chance to do a brave deed like Antonio's— a deed that even his big brother might admire. Of course, Miguel was too young to carry a gun, but you couldn't tell, his chance might come. There were always brave deeds waiting to be done by boys who were not afraid.

The sand-colored road on which they journeyed looked across cactus-studded fields on either hand to the far off mountains cut out of blue cardboard against the sky. The bright sunlight made everything shimmer in a kind of haze of dust and heat. That morning the road led down a long slope, across a stream, through a little valley and up another hill to a great plain. One of Uncle Mario's horsemen who was called Pancho rode ahead of the herd. He was as brown as leather and just as weather-beaten and tough. Colima, the second of the horsemen, was a slender young fellow with a curl in his hair. He followed the bronco herd and did most of the hard riding when it became necessary to bring back into line one of the horses that took a notion to break away. The last of this trio was Old Juan. He was the grizzly one, wrinkled and hard. He drove the provision wagon to which the burros were hitched. Another team of burros was tied to the back of the wagon.

Pancho and Old Juan were of Uncle Mario's age and both of them were silent mountain men who attended strictly to business and spoke only when it was absolutely necessary. Colima, on the other hand, was just over twenty. He loved to talk and sing, and he brought a guitar along. It was tucked away with the provisions and luggage.

Miguel and Uncle Mario rode side by side behind the herd. After them came the wagon drawn by the burros. Miguel's horse had an easy, smooth

walking gait and when noon came the boy was not tired
at all. Besides, there had been so many scrubby trees and
adobe houses on the landscape, so many goats and birds
looking for their homes, that the time passed swiftly, and
Miguel was surprised when Old Juan pulled the wagon
off the road, came to a stop in a clump of manzanita,
and suggested a little rest and something to eat.

"Well, I could stand it," Uncle Mario told him,
dismounting in the shade and stretching his legs.

There was water nearby, and already Pancho had
led the broncos to its edge. Miguel climbed down and
tied his horse to a sapling.

"Me for a wink of sleep," Colima laughed. He
took the bridle off his sweating horse, slapped the
animal's flanks and sent him down to the water to
refresh himself. The next minute he was stretched out
on the ground, his big sombrero shading his face.

"This is about the longest ride you ever had, isn't
it, Miguel?" Uncle Mario asked.

"Yes, but I'm not tired. I can keep on going and
going," Miguel assured him.

"Sure you can," his uncle smiled, "but rest and
good food won't do a young man any harm. What do
you say we help Old Juan get a fire going?"

It was no sooner said than done. Old Juan was
the cook for the outfit, the provision man. Miguel and
his uncle gathered a small heap of dead wood and brush
stalks, and the wrinkled old horseman went to work with
his frying pan and coffee pots. Before Colima could
finish his beauty nap, the cook twisted his foot to awaken
him, and offered him a tin cupful of coffee and a tin

plate piled high with a mixture of onions and eggs.

Riding gave you a good appetite. Miguel only realized how hungry he was after he commenced eating. The more onions and eggs he ate, the more his capacity seemed to become.

"I didn't know I was so hungry," he admitted, passing his tins back to Old Juan for the third time.

"That's what they call a coming appetite," his uncle laughed. "Not much at the start, but picking up as you go along. How about a song, Colima?"

"A song!" the young horseman exclaimed, washing down his bread with a gulp of coffee. "It's too early to sing. I can't sing till after dark."

"H'm," Pancho mumbled with a sly wink. "I know a bird like him. All time play and sing in moon-light! That's him all right. That Colima."

Colima laughed and continued to eat.

"Now it's me that's sleepy," Uncle Mario confessed. "Wake me up when you get your things together ready to strike out again, Juan."

When they were all through eating, Colima went down to the water to be near the herd and keep his eye on them. Old Juan washed out his cooking things and replaced them in the wagon. Then he went back to the manzanita clump and stretched himself on the ground for a late mid-day siesta such as Pancho and Uncle Mario were already enjoying. Miguel wasn't sleepy. He joined Colima.

The air was clear now. You could see for miles and miles. There were mountains in the far distance and a few hills nearby. A tiny thread of smoke could be seen curling upward from a dim, dark spot that looked like a village. This was toward the east and considerably off the road, so Miguel paid little attention to it at first. Still it was strange that no houses could be seen beyond the dark spot from which the smoke rose.

"What do you make of it?" he asked Colima.

"That smoke? Nothing. Maybe a fire."

That sounded very wise and yet very silly to Miguel. Colima was surely right about the fire. It was hard to imagine anything else causing smoke, but for some reason this did not satisfy Miguel.

"Looks funny to me," he said.

"Fires are everywhere," Colima laughed. "What's funny about them?"

"Bandits don't stop to build fires, do they?" Miguel asked suddenly.

"Bandits! What ever put that in your mind?"

Miguel told him about the attack on the train that had carried his brother to Mexico City.

"Everybody knows there are bandits up this way," he concluded.

"We're not near any railroad track," Colima assured him.

Miguel wondered if being away from the train tracks made any difference, but he did not say anything more about bandits. He didn't want to show fear. That was his resolution, and talking about bandits didn't help you much when you were determined to be brave. But Colima was more disturbed than he wanted to let on — for these were troubled times in the year 1915 and Mexico was a troubled land. Miguel saw the young man turn away and cross himself swiftly.

While the two were still together down by the water, Old Juan roused himself and began calling the other men. Miguel left Colima and untied his own horse. A moment of confusion followed with the others mounting and getting the big herd on the move again. The young broncos wanted to rebel, but they soon found they couldn't break away with seasoned horsemen like Pancho and Colima rounding them up and lashing their sides with the blacksnake whips they carried for the unruly ones. A few moments of this romping and rearing, then all of them got in order again and decided to follow the leader.

"After a day or two, when you get a little more riding under your belt, Miguel, I'll let you help Pancho and Colima run these wild jackrabbits down when they get to rip-tearing like that. There's another blacksnake whip in the wagon there."

"That's what I'm waiting for," Miguel said. Both of them became silent for a space. Then Miguel added, "Have you noticed that smoke across there?"

The uncle had not, and now that it was called to his attention, he was not inclined to make much of it. After all, there were many villages and many isolated lonely mud huts. A fire on the plain meant nothing. Miguel said no more about it. But later that day something happened that caused Uncle Mario and Colima as well as the other two men to think the second time about that tiny thread of smoke the boy had called to their attention.

The outfit made a good afternoon, covering

perhaps fifteen miles and came at length to a village on the top of a hill. A village of crooked cobbled stone streets and flat adobe houses. Most of the houses were a natural mud-gray, but some were painted bright pink or blue. The only thing that rose above the low houses was the white tower of the church, old and beautiful, supporting an enormous iron-green bell.

Uncle Mario ordered the outfit to stop, and he began passing a few friendly words with the mountain people who came out of their huts to stare at the unusually large herd of wild horses. An old barefoot woman tending a huge kettle over the fire in her yard offered the men something hot to eat, so they decided to accept. They did not get down from their saddles, however, because the broncos had to be watched. They were tired and restless at this hour, and there was no running water at hand to hold their interest. They nibbled what trash they saw on the ground and when they saw nothing better, they nibbled each other. This produced the usual kicking, rearing and running. But from the old woman the horsemen took the big tortillas filled with hot chili beans and enjoyed them very much.

Miguel liked them too, but he scarcely got started on his before he noticed a strange look come over his uncle's face.

"You were right, Miguel," Mario whispered.

"What?"

"See down there. They are following us. A host of them."

Sure enough, less than a mile behind on the road that had brought the outfit to this high village there was a detachment of straggling armed men. Miguel could see them distinctly at this moment. Their leader rode a horse, but the rest of them were on foot. He could even make out that the bandit company wore no shoes.

Miguel's teeth chattered.

"Follow me," Uncle Mario told him.

A moment later, without arousing the village folks or indicating to them what they had seen from the backs of their horses, Miguel and his uncle passed the warning to Colima and Pancho and Old Juan. The blacksnake whips of the horsemen snapped like pistol shots. A small-sized mutiny on the part of the beasts was quickly snuffed out, and the company started down the hill. Uncle Mario and Miguel were leading with the provision wagon following directly behind the herd. Bringing up the rear were Colima and Pancho.

A cold perspiration came over Miguel. Something inside his stomach began to flip over and over like a fish thrown out of water. Maybe that was the food he had just eaten at the village. Still he didn't remember any jumping beans in the tortillas the old woman had given them. Then why this terrible flipping up and down and over and over inside? Why this cold perspiration? Why did his teeth chatter even when he tried to grit them together?

There was a wagon path down the hill, and beyond there were other hills with small valleys folded between them. But the road the company had been following led another way. It descended the slope and came out on a plain that appeared to be many, many miles in length.

"They'll overtake us if we follow the road," Uncle

Mario said. "The burros can't run with the wagon, and the broncos will get out of control if we try to hurry them too fast."

"They all had guns," Miguel said. "All that I saw."

"Never mind," his uncle said. "Just take it easy and keep up with me."

Miguel's horse was still walking, but she was walking much faster than at any time earlier that day. Even at that, she was falling perhaps a length behind Uncle Mario's tall, chestnut horse. Behind these the two burros tied to the back of the wagon were almost under the feet of the excited broncos. Now and again Miguel found that he and his uncle and the wagon were surrounded by the hurrying broncos. Miguel cast swift glances over his shoulder every moment or two, but now trees and the slopes of the hill and the curve of the wagon path kept the village from view, and it was not possible to determine just how near the pursuers were behind them.

"We'll give them a better chase than they're looking for," Uncle Mario said, setting his jaw. "And maybe— maybe when it gets dark we can give them the slip."

Looking ahead, Miguel got a hint of what his uncle had in mind. He was at that moment cutting sharply toward the left, leaving the wagon path. The sun was dropping slowly out of sight. Vast shadows fell upon the hills. Further on rose other hills and still others beyond.

No more words were spoken. The soft thunder of the hurrying broncos echoed and re-echoed between the hills, however, and there wasn't a moment of silence.

Miguel's horse became damp with sweat. He discovered too, that the perspiration on his own body was warmer now. The flip-flopping in his stomach had become less annoying. He could still feel it once in a while, but it wasn't so steady.

The next thing he knew, Uncle Mario had reached the flat bed of a near-dry stream. His horse's feet were splashing in the small puddles of water. The wagon rocked along with difficulty. A bit later, when he felt he could risk it, Uncle Mario halted the outfit long enough to hitch the extra burros in front and add them to the team pulling the small provision wagon. This took only a minute or two; and since the wagon was not heavy, great advantage of speed was gained.

Miguel was not sure how long they continued to use that creek as a roadway and a guide, but he knew that when they finally turned away from the creek, night had fallen. The way had grown pitch dark.

"We must keep moving," Uncle Mario whispered. "We may have shaken them off, but the safest way is to keep moving, keep moving."

Chapter III
A Story Beneath the Stars

With the next day's journeying the bandits were safely eluded. They were left far behind, and twilight found Miguel, his uncle and the three swarthy horsemen surrounding a small red fire on a high plain. All of them were dog-tired after so many hours in the saddle. Miguel's legs were so stiff they seemed ready to crack. It did worlds of good to lie on the ground in the gathering darkness, to stretch his aching limbs and look up into the great bowl of golden stars overhead.

The evening meal had been eaten, but Old Juan had left the coffee pot on the coals so that they might all enjoy another cup later. Now the old fellow's eyes were closed as were those of his two companions.

"Why so silent tonight, Uncle Mario?" Miguel said suddenly.

"Oh, just thinking, Miguel." He paused a few seconds, then added, "There was a story in my mind."

"Nothing beats a story. What was it, Uncle Mario?"

"This country we've been crossing brought it to my mind early this afternoon," Uncle Mario said. "And tonight, with the sky so full of stars and the broncos feeding together out there, it comes back again."

"Tell it, Uncle Mario," Miguel urged. "Tell it to all of us."

The tall, slender, curly-haired Colima sat up suddenly and reached for his guitar.

"Si, Señor," he said, adjusting his saddle on the ground so as to rest his back against it. He began strumming softly. "Anybody likes a story," he added, "especially if it's about a horse."

"Fortunately, Colima, this is about a horse," Uncle Mario smiled.

The young Colima continued to strum gently. Pancho and Old Juan opened their eyes. Miguel sat up attentively, and Uncle Mario began the tale.

"It was in the days of our fathers, yes, our grandfathers," he began. "These plains and those that reach beyond them across the United States to Canada were familiar with the thunder of mighty herds in those days."

"Oh, I know— buffalo," Miguel said.

"Well, many of them were buffalo herds," Uncle Mario explained, "but there were also wild horses—mustangs—the ancestors of these little broncos of ours. The mustangs ran in somewhat smaller herds than the buffalo, but they kicked up more dust. They could run like the wind, and they were beautiful. What's more, they were smart—as most horses are—and they used their wits when the occasion arose.

"The mustangs, like our broncos, were smaller animals than work horses, but they were well-made, with trim legs, excellent heads and shoulders, long flowing manes, and tails that sometimes touched the ground. They were built for speed rather than brute strength, and they roamed hundreds and hundreds of miles across the plains without seeming to think anything of distance."

"And nobody bothered them?" Miguel asked.

"Oh, they were far too beautiful to go unmolested,"

Uncle Mario sighed. "They had always to be on the alert for mountain lions and other fierce animals. Thus they learned to avoid the trees from which beasts might pounce upon them. They found out that the mountains with their ravines and cliffs and overhanging rocks were unsafe. In this way the plains became their home, the plains on which the race belonged to the swift, rather than the strong—for nothing was swifter than the wild mustang in those days.

"It is true that the Indians learned to catch them and to train them to their use, but that is another story. I want to tell you about a horse that no Indian could catch, no white man, either. It was a white stallion, a leader of mustang herds, and a sort of king of wild horses. This great animal was seen by tribes as far north as Montana and as far south as these Serrano plains of ours. Sometimes this stallion was followed by half a dozen mares. Sometimes he was seen leading a herd of thousands of mustangs.

"No one ever had more than a fleeting glance at this wonderful creature. His instincts were so sharp and keen, he could detect the approach of a man long before the man came into view. He had a sense of danger that was astonishing even for a wild mustang. Always on these occasions he would give the warning to his companions and they would be off in a cloud of dust. Pursuit was useless. They were much too swift for that.

"When the Indians laid their traps for him, and put out food to entice the great white stallion, they would return to find the traps sprung, the food taken, but no wild horse. If there was no way to get the food without stepping into a noose or falling into a pit, the Indians would find that the mustangs had come with their leader, walked around and around the dangerous place—and then withdrawn leaving the bait untouched.

"Now, that was very different from the ordinary run of mustangs. The Indians could sometimes spring up suddenly on their own swift ponies, run down and overtake the half-grown mustang colts and throw ropes around their necks. Sometimes they could even catch a full-grown horse. Trapping the mustangs was not much of a problem for the shrewd red man. But this white stallion was not to be taken by any of these means. Season after season rolled past. The leaves came and the leaves went away. The beautiful white horse increased in age, and as he grew older he grew more cunning. The Indians talked about him a great deal, but they gave up the hope of ever capturing him.

"Then the white man came to the plains. The Indians told them the story of this leader of mustang herds. But the white pioneers, who had heard the same story told by different tribes of red men from Mexico to the border of Canada, found it hard to believe. They couldn't imagine a horse covering that much ground during his life, and they smiled and shook their heads when they listened to accounts of this animal's remarkable cunning. Later, however, some of the first of these pioneers saw for themselves.

"As the white stallion grew older, he became less afraid of man. Sometimes, followed by a dozen of his companions, he would come quite close to the log house of a pioneer family, lift his magnificent head in the air, inspect the odd premises, and then tossing his mane and turning swiftly, he would split the air with a great neigh and gallop off in a cloud of dust. Once it was said that a frontiersman took his musket down from the wall and fired a shot at the handsome mustang, but the bullet went wild. The white stallion had already commenced to zig-zag so cleverly that the man with the gun had no chance to make an effective shot.

Another time a woman of the frontier was digging potatoes in a patch in front of her cabin. She lifted her eyes and saw the white stallion standing only a few yards away. He showed no fear at all. The woman later said that she felt sure she could have gone to him and patted his nose had she not been so astonished that she cried out suddenly. Even then, however, the stallion was not dismayed. He turned slowly and trotted back to the small herd that waited for him in full view on the prairie, not more than a quarter of a mile away.

"A few more seasons passed. Snow spread a blanket over the plains in winter and then removed it in the spring so that the prairie grass could come up and grow. Wild geese went south and returned, went south and returned again, as first one year, then two years, and then three years passed. The white stallion remained a great leader of mustangs. He lost none of his proud beauty, though he approached the age when most horses are considered old. He lost none of his amazing swift-ness. He lost none of his shrewd cunning and his sharp instincts, but he grew more gentle.

"Yes," Uncle Mario reflected, "gentle is the word, as you will see. For about this time a frontiersman—of whom there were more and more living on the plains—sent his little daughter to the mill with a sack of corn. Now, I'll have to tell you, Miguel, that in those times the early settlers of the plains had a way of tossing a sack of corn across a horse's back and then putting a child on top of the sack. They would use a very tame horse for this, and the child would be pretty sure to reach the mill without mishap simply by keeping the horse in the middle of the wagon path. At the mill the corn would be ground. When it was ground, the corn would get more air between the particles. That meant that one sack of corn made more than one sack of meal. The miller would fill up the original sack with meal, however, and keep the rest for himself as his toll or commission for his work.

"Well, in those times, far up north of the border, there was much work to be done by settlers on their plots of ground, and most of them could not always spare the time to go to mill. If they had a child, as had the farmer in this story, they would simply put the sack of corn on the horse, the child on the sack, and send the young one off to the mill alone. There were dangers, as you must have guessed, because all the Indians had not yet made peace with the pioneer families. The roads were no more than faint trails and there was always the possibility of getting lost.

"This is just what happened on the day when the white stallion had his greatest adventure. One chilly autumn day, a little golden-haired girl reached the mill safely, riding on a sack of corn that had been placed on the back of a limping old farm horse. When the corn was ground and the sack replaced by the miller, the little girl noticed clouds swiftly scudding up the sky. She felt chill winds blowing from the north. How much better to be at home, if there was going to be a storm, she thought. Guiding the old animal into the way, she promptly started the five-mile return journey. The miller must have noticed the gathering clouds too. He came to the gate and urged the golden-haired child not to waste any time and to keep the old horse moving as fast as he could go on his lame foot.

"But the child soon realized that she would not be able to get home before the snow commenced falling, no matter how she hurried. The first flakes came down when she was scarcely out of sight of the mill. They came down slowly at first, then more fell. Soon the air was full of them, so full you could scarcely see ahead. It was not long before the wagon path was lost completely and the old horse began to stumble and grope his way. He turned to the left and he turned to the right as the snow blew in his face. He thrashed his way through thickets and groves. He went down slopes and crossed small creeks. When the snow finally stopped falling, neither the old lame horse nor the poor child had the slightest idea where they were or which way they should turn. The little girl began to cry."

Uncle Mario's voice broke off suddenly. Colima's strumming stopped; his hand hung limp on the guitar as the three horsemen and Miguel waited eagerly for the rest of the story.

"And then?" the guitarist asked.

"Yes, yes, go on, Uncle Mario," Miguel urged.

"Please don't stop."

But Uncle Mario would not be hurried. He waited a long moment, his eyes nearly closed as he reflected upon the old story.

"Night fell upon the snow-covered land," he said finally. "The lame old horse was worn out. The child by then had cried till she couldn't cry any more. She felt sleepy, too. When the faithful, but played out old animal stopped under a big tree, she did not kick his sides or try to make him go any further. Instead, she leaned forward on the big sack of meal, closed her eyes and went to sleep.

"How long she slept there she did not know, but when she opened her eyes finally, she was surprised to discover that her old horse was moving again. A second later she saw that another horse was just ahead, a lovely white creature, beautiful beyond words in the moonlight. Across the snow he led the way, pausing now and again to wait for the poor limping old farm horse to catch up. He was a gentle thing, that lovely white stallion, and more than once he turned around and brought his head very close to the head of the old farm horse as if he was whispering encouragement and comfort.

"The child was happy and no longer worried. She felt much rested after her little nap, but she began to wonder now just where the white horse was lead-ing them. Wherever it was, she was sure, her old horse seemed to have no worries. He followed along with complete confidence. Hours passed. Then just before the dawn, the child began to see things that looked

familiar to her in the moonlight. Finally the bright
orange windows of a cabin came into view, and she
realized that she was home again.

"Mother!" the child cried. A door opened and
a stream of golden light fell across the snow. The white
stallion stepped aside to allow the miserable, weary
old horse and the happy child to pass, then he turned
and trotted away to join his mates somewhere on the
prairie. The marvelous leader of the mustangs had led
the lame old horse and the golden-haired child back to
their home and perhaps saved them both from death
on the great wild prairie in the snow."

So that was the story. Miguel liked it enormously.
He could see in his mind the rejoicing in the frontier
cabin when the little girl rejoined the father and mother
who had by then, perhaps given up in despair the hope
of finding their child again. Uncle Mario didn't have
to add that part. Miguel knew, because he knew how it
would be in his house should he be lost. He knew how
his own mother was worried even now because he was
further away from home than he had ever been before.

"Ah," he said softly, when his uncle had ceased
talking. "That's what I like about horses. They're
so wonderful."

"Not all of them are as fine as the white stallion
who led the mustangs, but they are grand animals just
the same. I like them, too."

"Whatever became of the white stallion?"
Miguel asked.

"Nobody knows," Uncle Mario smiled. "This
story and many, many others like it are told. Nobody

knows what became of him. Some say he was last seen in Serrano. Some say he could be as terrible as he could be kind, and that he was known to come back and kill cruel men who attempted to take his life by shooting at him. They say he was too proud to turn his back and kick with his hind feet, but instead rose on his hind legs and struck his enemies mighty blows from his front hoofs. Many people tell stories about the white stallion. He must have been indeed a marvelous horse. Still nobody knows just what became of him. Some say one thing, some another."

"I hear those stories," Old Juan grunted. "Lots of times I hear them."

"Me, too," Pancho murmured sleepily. "That white stallion you tell—wonderful mustang."

"Now Miguel, let's get some sleep," Uncle Mario said. "Early start tomorrow, you know."

All five of them stretched out on the blankets they had spread on the ground. Miguel closed his eyes, but he did not let them stay closed. He kept peeking at the stars overhead and thinking about the white stallion and the golden-haired child. He wondered what his mother and father and little Angelita would be doing about this hour and how they would take the news should they hear that he, like the child in the story, had been lost some place on the wide open spaces of the plains or on the great desert beyond. All the sleep left his eyes when he thought of things like these; but when Colima began soft playing on his guitar again, Miguel lost his fears and commenced to dream.

Presently he was fast asleep.

CHAPTER IV
Cactus Country
❧

The next morning the herd was on the move
again. All along the line the lively young broncos were
biting and kicking each other playfully, lingering
behind occasionally, running ahead, breaking away,
and in general making life exciting for the horsemen.
Miguel rode beside his uncle most of the time and
began to feel very proud of himself. He even began to
take a hand in the managing of the herd, and more than
once that day it fell to him to run down a colt that took
a notion to kick up his heels and dart across the sandy
plain alone. The first time he attempted it, the boy's
heart pounded hard. He feared that he might not
be able to overtake the frisky young bronco or, having
overtaken him, that he might not be able to head him
back toward the herd. But the chase turned out to
be easier than Miguel expected. His own horse could
easily outrun the bronco, and the young colt was soon
convinced that he had better come back and behave
himself. After that first test, Miguel felt more sure of
himself and his horse. By afternoon he had straightened
out half a dozen broncos that tried to get out of line.

At noon the men lay on the ground smoking and
relaxing from a morning in the saddle. Miguel, who
didn't feel tired, wandered off alone and saw a chaparral
cock, a speckled thing with a ruffled crest on his head,
run from under a clump of cactus. The bird paused
long enough to let Miguel see the lizard in its mouth,
then turned and fled, running at a blinding speed. An
hour or two later, when the herd was on its way again,

the broncos aroused some wild boars that had been feeding on mesquite beans. The boars showed their long teeth angrily and offered to stand their ground. When Pancho drew his pistol and fired, however, one of them ran into the brush screaming, and the others scurried after him. For the rest of the day the journey was uneventful.

The next evening two small snookum bears climbed into a tree overhead and watched Miguel and the men mischievously. They were gentle little fellows with tiny ears and funny, long snouts, and Miguel knew, as did the men, that they would do no real harm. The next morning, however, he was awakened by the shouts of Juan.

"What's the trouble, Juan?' Uncle Mario asked without opening his eyes.

"Malo, malo," the old horseman complained. He was so exasperated he could scarcely talk. "Trouble. You say right. Muy malo. All the cornmeal's gone. Those snookum bears—they do it. Now look at them in that tree. They so full they sleep all time. You can't wake them with stick."

"I saw them last night," Miguel said.

"Well, we can't blame the bears. We should have put the stuff away better. Besides, we can get more meal at the next village," said Uncle Mario.

With that, all was forgiven where the little bears were concerned, and the outfit commenced another day of dusty plodding under a dazzling sun. Miguel began to pay more attention to the clusters of little adobe huts they passed along the way, to the bright-eyed, half-naked children of the mountain people and to the beautiful kera-kera birds that circled overhead or stood looking very dignified on the stones of the hillside. He kept his eyes open for rattlesnakes curled in the sand. But even with such things as these to make the journey exciting, the days began to seem longer and longer, and Miguel wondered how many more days it would take them to reach Los Angeles.

"Are we halfway?" he asked his uncle one day as they jogged along in the late afternoon.

"Halfway? No, not halfway yet, but we've covered some of the hardest country. Things will brighten up soon," Uncle Mario assured him.

The next day Miguel got to thinking about the bandits and wondered if the danger was entirely passed. He had seen no trace of them since that first chase through the valley, and it seemed to him rather odd that neither Uncle Mario nor the horsemen seemed to consider the lawless bands of real danger any longer.

When Miguel asked about it, Colima laughed.

"Bandits!" he exclaimed. "No bandits, Miguel. Don't you know where you are?

"No, where are we?"

"We're in Arizona," Uncle Mario explained. "We've crossed the border."

"Back there where you stopped to talk to the soldiers?"

"I thought you knew what it was all about."

"But it doesn't look like the United States to me," Miguel said. "It doesn't look any different from Mexico."

"Los Angeles will look different," the uncle assured him. "Along the border here I suppose both sides do look pretty much alike."

So this was the United States, Miguel thought. How his mother and father would laugh when he told them that he had been in the States several hours before he knew it. But whoever heard of such a United States as this, with cactus everywhere you looked, with yucca plants and scrubby trees and sagebrush and jimson weed till you couldn't rest. With dove-colored hills against the horizon, with coyotes slinking through the brush—with all such as this, there was surely little indeed that wasn't exactly like the state of Sonora in Mexico. Come to think about it though, Miguel was rather glad to find Arizona much like his native state. He didn't feel strange and out-of-place as he had feared and expected he would feel. Indeed, it was almost as if he had been at home, just a few miles from his mother and father.

A few more days passed. Then one evening when they were having supper around the sagebrush fire that Old Juan had kindled, Miguel discovered something that looked like fairy lights in the distance. They were off to the north, and they twinkled brighter than stars.

"Look, Uncle Mario," he exclaimed happily.

"Ah, a city," Uncle Mario cried. "Perhaps Phoenix. But we have not time to stop. We won't even pass through it."

Miguel was mightily impressed as he gazed off toward the magical dancing lights, and he began to feel that they were coming to something that was different indeed from anything he had ever before seen.

"Halfway yet?" he asked breathlessly.

"Oh yes, a good halfway," his uncle mused.

That night Miguel was wakeful. Twice he rose on his elbow and saw those lights still burning brightly. The next morning, when they could no longer be seen, the outfit got an early start and Miguel began to look ahead to other things.

"Long pull, eh?" Colima said, making a cigarette in one hand as the horses jogged along.

Miguel nodded.

"You're right," he agreed. "Long pull."

"We can make it, though."

"Sure, we can make it. I'm not tired," the boy said.

Dust rose from the heels of the horses and from the wheels of the provision wagon. Miguel saw it drifting away like a pink cloud on the breeze. It was good to be riding a horse on a bright day like this, across miles and miles of cactus country. It made you feel big and strong and free—like a man. Miguel liked it.

Chapter V

A River Crossing

❧

Until they reached the Colorado River, a swift, muddy stream, running along the state line and dividing California from Arizona, Miguel had little contact with the North American people he met along the way. Here, however, there was a surprise or two in store for him.

Three days had passed since Miguel saw the lights of that city. Most of the way had been desert, dry, dusty, cactus-covered desert, and the herd had suffered between green spots. Rattlesnakes seemed to be curled under almost every stone, and they had to be careful to keep from stepping on one at night when they made camp. So it was with a sigh of relief that he came over the last knoll and looked down on the flashing water of the river in the sunset.

Miguel was now doing a man's job with the herd, riding along on one side and making himself responsible, just as Colima was on the other side. Juan was riding a horse now too. He had grown tired of the wagon and prevailed upon Uncle Mario to drive for a few days while he took to his saddle again.

"I knew you would like it, Miguel," Uncle Mario said, pointing at the stream from his seat in the wagon.

"Do we stop here?" the boy asked.

"Oh no, we'll see if we can't get across first. See the green stuff on the other side?"

Uncle Mario whistled to Pancho and waved his hand toward the river, ordering the lead horseman to move ahead. A few moments later the whole herd, the

saddled beasts, and the wagon were on the bank of the
stream and wondering what to do next.

There was reason to wonder, too. Miguel discovered suddenly that there was something odd about the
Colorado river at this point. On the east side, where
they were, there was a high, stony bank above the water
that broke off abruptly with a dizzy, swirling current
racing down below in a deep channel. Across the stream
on the other side of the river it was very different. There
the level, red land sloped gently down to the edge of the
stream. The water was slow and lapped the shore softly.
On the other side, it appeared, one could wade out into
the stream gradually. From the east bank, where the
herd now stood, nothing like that was possible. The
best you could do from this side was to jump or fall off
the bank into the perilously swift part of the stream.

"Guess we can't wade across," Miguel said, laughing.

"Bet your boots, we can't," his uncle called from
the wagon. "Can't swim it either. Look at that current.
Say, that's a wild baby, if you ask me."

Colima looked puzzled.

"It makes a pretty noise, too, but I'm thinking about
getting across. Did that ever cross your mind, Señor?"

Miguel turned and saw his uncle laughing heartily.

"Oh, yes, Colima," the big man said. "That crossed
my mind. But if you will trouble yourself to look up the
river there, you'll see why I'm not too upset about it."

Sure enough there was something on the bank
a few hundred yards up stream, but Miguel, when he
turned, couldn't exactly make out what it was. He followed
Colima and Pancho, however, when they struck out in that

direction, one leading and the other driving the herd as they went. A closer view made everything plain. A sort of landing had been arranged at a spot where the east bank was not as high as in other places. There was a large, raft-like thing floating on the water. It was tied by a pulley to a cable that had been stretched from one bank to the other. Nearby a shack and a barn had been built.

"Some people make funny thing," Pancho grunted, looking at the make-shift boat.

"A right good ferry, if you ask me, Pancho," Uncle Mario said. "If it gets us across, what more can we ask?"

Pancho smiled faintly, shrugged his shoulders and started down to the tiny landing place. By that time the noise had aroused a man in the shack. He came out smoking a pipe, and Uncle Mario got down from the wagon and met him.

At first Miguel didn't understand what they said to each other, because they spoke a language he hadn't yet learned—English—but presently the boatman indicated that he knew Spanish, too, so Uncle Mario talked to him in his native language.

"Passel of broncos you've got there," the man observed.

"Quite a few," Uncle Mario said. "Can you get us across?"

"Surest thing you know, friend. That's what I'm here for."

A price was agreed upon, and the boatman returned to his shack to finish the dinner he had left on his plate. While he was in the hut the horsemen unhitched the burros, and rolled the wagon down to the landing point. When the boatman returned, he was followed by a freckled boy with carrot-colored hair. The men went to work immediately.

It was slow business because the old raft-like ferry could carry only a small load at a time, besides, it had to be poled part of the way. In the midst of the current it was flung about and tossed so roughly there was a problem of keeping everything aboard, but once past midstream it slowed down and had to be laboriously helped along with a pole.

While this was going on, the American boy came near and began to inspect the herd.

"Lots of horses you've got," he said in Spanish.

Miguel nodded.

"Quite a few," he said.

"Where do you come from?"

Before he knew it, Miguel was giving the American boy a full account of the journey, decorating the story a little where he thought a few additions would help to make it more interesting. He told about the bandits, but instead of making it clear that it was a dried-up stream they had followed through the little valley, he gave the red-haired boy the impression that all of them had plunged into a full-sized river. He told of being thrown from his horse and swimming most of the way across. He also added something about shooting it out with the bandits from the opposite bank. Why he told all this extra detail, he didn't know, but it just seemed to fit in nicely with the story, and the American boy showed a great deal of interest.

"Didn't any of you get shot?"

"Oh, I got my hat shot off my head," Miguel told him. "Another time, when I was lying on my stomach, shooting from behind a rock, I put my hat on a stick and held it out so the bandits would think it was my head. One of them shot it down. That was about all."

"Where's your gun now?"

"My gun? Lost. Swimming that river, you know."

"I thought you were already across the river."

"We shot it out with them before we came to the river, too."

"Gee, that was a close shave. What's your name?"

Miguel told him and found out that the boatman's boy was named Larry. By then, the ferry was back and ready for another load. It was arranged for Miguel to linger behind with Colima and keep the broncos together till they could be transported. Some of the horses did not want to get on the raft, but gradually they yielded to persuasion. Pancho stayed on the raft with the ferryman and went back and forth as the herd was transported. Uncle Mario and Old Juan remained on the west bank after crossing with the first load.

It took a long time. The sun sank rapidly. Miguel and Larry continued to entertain each other with hair-raising stories. Finally, just as twilight commenced to deepen, the last load went across and with it Miguel and Colima and their saddle horses. Larry, the boatman's boy, came too. There was plenty of room this time. Larry just came for the ride.

"This is the first time I've been across today," he explained.

The boatman shoved off and the raft was hurled by the current. It strained on its cable like a kite on a string. Then suddenly it gave a queer lurch tilting one side much higher than the other. Miguel who had been standing near the edge suddenly realized that he was not standing at all, but flying. A moment later he was not even flying. He was floundering in the cold, rushing water and more inclined to sink than to stay on the surface.

Larry laughed, thinking that maybe the young Mexican had leaped into the water just for a swim. Colima began to look dismayed. The boatman, busy with his pole, was looking the other way. Miguel caught a glimpse of the three as he rose to the surface. Then, realizing that he was sinking and that nobody was getting ready to do anything about it, he cried out pitifully.

"Help! I can't swim," he called. "Help!"

Larry was more perplexed than ever. He wrinkled up the freckles on his nose and looked first at his father and then at Colima. On the west side of the river Uncle Mario caught a glimpse of his nephew in the water and commenced to wave his arms excitedly.

"Hurry up there, you two," the boatman shouted roughly. "If neither one of you is going to do anything, take this pole and I will."

"But he told me he swam a river twice as big as this one," Larry protested.

"Forget it," his father cried. "Can't you see he can't swim?"

With that Colima kicked off his boots, threw off his sombrero, and made a dive. At the same moment Larry, who was already barefooted, hit the water neatly.

A moment of excited tugging followed, a moment in which the two swimmers, the boy, and the young man managed to drag the frightened and half-strangled Miguel out of the swift current and into the calmer water beyond. Getting him back on the ferry was out of the question. They had drifted too far down stream while making the rescue. But presently Miguel felt his feet drag on the soft mud of the riverbed, and he commenced walking with the help of the two others.

On the shore, cold, ashamed of himself, and still feeling terrible, Miguel scarcely heard the rapid words of his uncle and the men. He knew, however, when they peeled his wet clothing off, and he felt the heat of the blaze when Old Juan got a fire going. By that time night had fallen.

A silence fell upon the group. The broncos, after three days of scant pickings, were nearly knee-deep in grass and quickly making up for lost time. Old Juan commenced to rattle his pots and pans.

"Miguel told me he could swim," Larry said suddenly.

Miguel turned over so the others could not look into his face. He felt terrible.

"H'm," Uncle Mario murmured. "Making up things, hunh? Well, you see how far a lie will get you. Just an inch from drowning."

Miguel was so ashamed he had to fight hard to keep from crying.

"That's what I tell you sometimes, too, Larry," the ferryman said. "The main trouble with lying is that it's so stupid."

Larry took a moment to turn his father's words over in his mind.

"But Miguel wasn't really lying," he protested. "He was just kind of talking up a dream."

"Making up a story," the boatman said.

"It was a good story," Larry said.

The men all laughed.

"Mighty lucky he's still not making up a dream, too," Colima said, wringing the water out of his own shirt.

Miguel was glad that at least Larry held no blame against him. When the ferryman and the boy started toward the river raft again, he rose on his elbow and tried to thank Larry for helping to pull him out of the water.

"That other river was wider than this one," he insisted again. "But there wasn't any water in it. I made a mistake. Some of that other stuff I told you was a mistake, too. But we did see some bandits."

Chapter VI
Bow and Arrow

When Miguel woke up next morning, the first thing he saw was a small company of blanketed American Indians standing beside their horses on the opposite bank of the river. They were waiting for the ferryman to come out of the hut and give them a lift across the swift stream. As they waited, they stood very proud and dignified in the pearly morning light, and all seemed particularly intent upon Uncle Mario's group that was just beginning to stir on the opposite bank.

"Down from the Navajo reservation, I suppose," Uncle Mario said, wiping the sleep out of his eyes.

Pancho grunted, rolled up his pants, waded out and began washing his face in the muddy river water.

"I know. I see them long time ago. Long time ago when I make this trip. They my friends, those Indians."

"Look at their blankets," Miguel said. "Look, Colima."

The young, hard-sleeping Colima had not yet finished his final nap, but he rolled over when he heard his name called.

"The devil with blankets," he said, "Don't talk to me about blankets this early in the morning. I'm sleepy."

"Too bad," Old Juan said. "All night play guitar, sing. No good. Too late now. Get up. Find more wood for fire. See?"

"Aw, jump in the river," Colima said, stretching his legs and yawning. "I need rest."

"You not need rest."

"All he needs is some cold water to wake him up," Uncle Mario said. "Get a bucket, somebody."

"Never mind," Colima cried. "Don't drown me. I'm getting up."

By this time Miguel was stirring briskly, pulling on his shoes, washing his face and combing his hair. By the time the company sat down around the fire, the ferryman was out in his shirtsleeves, making ready to bring the Indians across.

The blanketed figures meant no harm, of course, and when they finally reached the west bank of the river with their sleek little spotted ponies, Miguel saw that they were gentler men than Pancho and Old Juan. Their skin was a bright copper, while the horsemen of Uncle Mario were duller in color and more leather-brown. None of those Indians from the reservations had mustaches like the Mexicans.

The leader of the little band of Indians, a heavy, thin-lipped man, mounted his horse as soon as he had led the animal off the raft. He rode over to where the fire of Old Juan was crackling, exchanged a few grunts with the men and stood looking down on them from his mount. After a long, uncomfortable pause, he beckoned to Miguel with his hand. The boy came toward him slowly.

"You good boy," the Indian said without a shadow of a smile. "I give you something. Here, take this. You like it?"

As he spoke, he opened his blanket, brought out what looked at first to be quite an ordinary stick.

"Thank you," Miguel said, accepting it with a

puzzled look on his face.

He couldn't imagine why the Indian seemed to take so much pride in offering him a stick that had been well-trimmed and carved a bit at each end, but that was otherwise most unremarkable.

The heavy-set Indian saw his bewilderment.

"Much good stick, I give you," he assured the boy. "Make fine bow and arrow. See?"

"Oh, yes, now I understand. Just what I want."

Pancho and Colima and Uncle Mario expressed admiration for the gift. Presently they were in conversation with the Indians and had explained their journey and asked a pack of questions on their own part. They learned that the Indians had friends down the river a few miles. They never had to hunt for their food on the reservation. Life was different now, but it was still fun to make bows and arrows. The stick which the leader had just given to Miguel had been found near the road as the little group of men trotted along in the gray light of dawn. The leader had intended it for one of his own grandchildren, but Miguel looked to him like such a fine boy that he had changed his mind.

A few more grunts were exchanged, hands were raised stiffly, and the reservation Indians were off, following the course of the stream. Presently they disappeared.

Breakfast was soon over, and Uncle Mario's outfit was ready to move again. Larry and his father came to see them off.

"Coming back this way?" Larry asked Miguel.

"Yes, sir, I think so."

"Right smart desert you got ahead of you," the ferryman said.

Uncle Mario nodded.

"Yes, that's about all there is between here and Mecca. And there's more beyond," he said.

"Well, hope you don't run into no sandstorms."

"Thanks. I hope we don't, too."

Larry turned to Miguel again and asked, "What's so wonderful out that way anyhow?"

"I don't know," Miguel shrugged. "We want to sell the horses in Los Angeles. That's where my Aunt Chona lives."

"Oh, I see."

"Goodbye," Miguel said, swinging into his saddle like a regular horseman.

"So long," Larry called. "See you when you come back."

"Sure, I hope so."

Before the first hour had passed, the outfit had reached the top of the mesa. Miguel noticed that the long, hard journey was having a quieting effect upon the broncos. They were less anxious to break away from the herd and dash off alone. They were feeling good after the fine feeding of the past night, but they were well-behaved. It was no job at all to look after them.

Old Juan nodded in the wagon, a cigarette hanging from his lips. Colima and Pancho rode along in silence. Suddenly Miguel noticed that Uncle Mario had stopped his horse and was looking back. The boy turned to see what had attracted his attention.

To Miguel's surprise, they were now several

hundred feet higher than the river. It was possible to see the twisting course of the stream for many miles to the south. To the north, mountains arose to cut off the view there. That was the direction from which the reservation Indians had come. All along the river the land was green, but off in the distance, either way you looked, there was nothing but desert and cactus country.

"Well," Uncle Mario smiled, "take a good look at it. Might be the last water we see for a good while."

"We can't keep going without water, can we?"

"Oh, the canvas bottles are full— enough to last us a day or two. And Juan filled two barrels for the herd. Not much for this many horses, but it should last us till we come to the first well."

"But there are some wells?"

"Two or three between here and Mecca. The biggest danger is losing the road. A sandstorm is likely to cover it."

"Gee, I hope we don't run into anything like that."

"Well, maybe we'll be lucky. Now you'd better dash up there and help Colima keep the broncos together."

Miguel rode past the wagon, caught up with the herd and took his place across from Colima. Pancho, following the twisting wagon trail across the sandy country, led the way barely a quarter of a mile ahead of the lumbering old wagon that brought up the rear. The sun grew hot. When noon came there was no tree or any other shade in sight. When they stopped, Miguel crawled under the wagon to eat his lunch and stretch out on the sand.

He was fastening a string to his new bow when he noticed wagons approaching from the other direction. Miguel crawled from under the wheels and looked. Yes, there were two wagons. They seemed to be prairie schooners with dull-colored tops, but they were still some distance away, so Miguel sat down again with the others and waited for them to draw near.

The wagons turned out to be a company of gypsies. A woman so fat, and dressed in so many colors that she looked like a great big pincushion, sat in the front seat of the first wagon. Beside her, holding the reins, was a thin dark-haired man with a face that reminded Miguel of an eagle. He wore large earrings. Behind this old couple in the wagon stood several younger women and little girls. The little girls were dressed just like the older women and would have looked like pincushions too had they been fatter.

The second wagon was driven by a very stout man with a crimson girdle around his waist, a green handkerchief tied around his head, and large silver buckles on his shoes. Beside him sat a half-grown boy, two or three years older than Miguel.

At first the company of strange people did not seem anxious to talk to Uncle Mario and his men. But, after hesitating a moment, Uncle Mario went over to the wagon where the thin man was sitting with his brown fluffy wife and started a conversation. A moment later the boy climbed down from the second wagon and came over to where Miguel was standing.

"Where'd you get that," he asked, pointing to the bow.

Miguel explained.

"Just got it today. An Indian gave it to me."

"Where are the arrows?"

"Haven't got any yet."

"Wait, I got some."

The gypsy boy went back to his wagon and returned with a bow and arrow of his own.

"Can yours shoot this high?" he said, aiming at the sky and drawing the bow.

When the arrow descended after a flight of a hundred or more feet, Miguel commenced to doubt that his would do as well. But he accepted the arrow the gypsy boy offered, placed it against the string and slowly took aim upward. As he drew the cord, he noticed that three small girls in the back of the first wagon were watching him. They had stopped paying attention to the conversation of the older folks to watch the shooting.

Miguel released the arrow. It sprang from the bow beautifully. Up it went — up, up, higher and higher. Miguel's eyes sparkled brightly as they followed its flight, for it was easy to see that it had gone much higher than the gypsy boy's shot.

What a marvelous bow, Miguel thought. The old Indian had indeed given him a priceless gift. Why, a bow that would shoot an arrow that high could be used for hunting. It could be used to protect the herd. If a mountain lion should attack a colt, a shot from this bow might make him change his mind. Buzzard hawks and rabbits would have no chance at all against such a weapon. All Miguel would need now would be arrows.

"Say," the gypsy boy said, "that was pretty good."

Miguel thought it was not pretty good, but very good.

"Yes," he said, "It'll do even better when I get used to it."

"Here, you shoot one arrow while I shoot the other. Both at the same time. In that way we can see which really goes the highest."

"All right," Miguel agreed confidently.

The boys aimed together.

"Ready — go!"

The arrows sprang upward, together. For an instant they rose side by side. Then one began to slow down as the other continued to mount.

"Look at mine," Miguel shouted happily. "Gee, look, it's still going up."

"Where?" the gypsy boy asked.

"Where? Where is it?" the little girls called. "I can't see it anymore."

Miguel could say nothing, because he too had lost sight of the swift arrow. When it returned to view again, he felt proud enough to burst. Think of it! Out of sight! A bow that would shoot an arrow so high the eye could not follow it. Too grand to be true.

"Out of sight! What do you think of that?" he said.

The gypsy boy lowered his eyes. He didn't seem pleased. Again Miguel shot an arrow upward, and again it disappeared for a swift moment in the blue. Then he called his uncle and Colima and showed them. They were both mightily impressed, but soon turned away for another conversation with the older gypsies, so the two boys returned to their shooting. But the gypsy boy grew more and more displeased with Miguel's superior bow.

"Think you're smart, don't you?" he said suddenly.

Miguel was too surprised to answer right away. After a moment he turned to his companion sharply.

"Here's your arrow," he said. "Take it, if that's the way you feel."

The boy thought for a moment.

"Not even going to let me shoot your bow once— after me letting you use my arrows? You're a bum sport."

"You didn't ask me to shoot it," Miguel said, "But you can shoot it." He handed his bow to the gypsy.

Casting his eyes low, glancing first out of one corner and then the other, the boy began to draw Miguel's bow while holding his own between his knees. Miguel thought he saw some kind of devilment in the bigger boy's eyes, but he couldn't imagine what the fellow was up to. Harder and harder the gypsy boy drew on the bow.

"Why don't you let it go?" Miguel cried suddenly. "That's drawn far enough."

"I'm going to make it shoot high! I'm going to make it shoot real high," the boy said dully.

"Stop!" Miguel yelled, "That's enough. You'll break it. Stop!"

At that moment it happened. The bow cracked. The gypsy boy gave a harsh little laugh.

"Wonder what made it do that," he grinned. "I wasn't pulling on it hard."

Miguel felt sick at heart but something within him wouldn't let him cry. Instead, he suddenly flew into

the other boy with both fists, catching the little gypsy by surprise.

"Hey, what's going on there?" Uncle Mario called.

Miguel couldn't answer. He was too busy using his fists. The other boy was using his, too. But Miguel was so angry the blows he received didn't hurt. All he could think of was that fine bow the old Indian had given him, the bow that would shoot an arrow so high it went out of sight, and the boy who had broken it just because his own couldn't match it.

The fat gypsy on the wagon seat lit his pipe. He didn't even seem to be interested in the fight. Uncle Mario and Colima, however, came over and took Miguel by the shoulders.

"Hold on," Colima said, "Somebody'll get hurt here if you don't look out."

"Is that the way you make friends with strangers, Miguel?" Uncle Mario asked kindly.

Miguel pointed to the broken bow on the ground.

"He did it," he said. "He did it on purpose."

"Aw, I didn't pull it hard," the gypsy boy sneered. "It just wasn't any good."

Miguel noticed that the boy's lip had been cut by a blow.

"Well now, fighting won't fix it," Uncle Mario said. "Let's move on."

The old woman who looked like a pincushion beckoned to the men with her hand.

"Come here. I'll tell your fortune," she said.

Uncle Mario and Colima shook their heads and climbed into their saddles.

"I'll sell you something pretty," the eagle-faced man suggested. "Come see. I've got it in my pocket here."

"No, thanks," Uncle Mario said, turning his back on them.

Miguel left the scene of the fight hesitantly. He would have enjoyed a chance to finish what he had begun, but the gypsy boy seemed to have had all he wanted of Miguel's fists for he was already climbing over the wheel of the second wagon and up onto the seat. Presently the gypsies cracked their whips and their wagons got under way again on the sandy path. Miguel climbed into his own saddle.

"That was a mean trick," Uncle Mario said, as they rode along. "That boy had no reason to break your bow. But it will teach you to be more careful of the strangers you meet. Not all of them are like Larry."

"Why did you stop me?" Miguel asked. "I would have given him something to remember."

"You gave him enough," the uncle chuckled. "I hated to stop you. I like a good fight as much as anybody. But fighting never settles anything. Sometimes it can't be helped, but it doesn't do any good. Why, if I'd let you two go on, those men might have dipped in. Then I would have had to take a hand. No telling what it might have led to. The bow was a good one, but it wouldn't be worth all that."

Miguel began to think that perhaps his uncle was right. He gave his horse a prod and rode up alongside the herd. Some of the broncos were getting out of line on his side. He nudged one or two of them, snapped a small whip at the others, and in a few seconds they were behaving themselves again. Far away behind him Miguel saw the gypsy wagons disappearing in a cloud of dust.

Chapter VII
So Far To Go

Before the sun disappeared that evening, they
came to a green spot on the desert. Pancho, riding
far ahead of the others, turned his horse suddenly,
raised his hand and pointed to a hut surrounded by
scrubby trees. A moment later Miguel saw the wooden
framework of a rude well.

They rested on the sand about a stone's throw
from the hut, and Miguel gathered brushwood for Old
Juan's cooking fire while his uncle and the other two
horsemen drew water from the well, a bucket at a time
for the saddle horses and the broncos.

That night the pickings were scanty for the herd
on the grassless sand, and they were frequently fretful
and ill-tempered. But shortly after dawn the company
was on the move again. The way was dull and tedious
now. All day long there was nothing to see but desert.
Sometimes it was flat, sometimes it was rolling with
dunes, sometimes it was rugged and dark, sometimes it
was soft and white, but always, all day long, it was desert.
Sand, sand, sand.

There were a few low hills, but nothing but cactus
grew on them. Rattlesnakes and lizards were the only
animals Miguel saw. Now and then a bird soared high
overhead avoiding the burning heat of the sand perhaps.
Sometimes Miguel saw bones on the desert, the dried
bones of dead animals. Once he noticed a flock of buz-
zards swarming over the carcass of a dead horse. Another
time he saw a broken cart that had been abandoned by
its owner many miles from the nearest green spot. Then

toward the next evening they came upon a man with a donkey.

The man told Uncle Mario that he was a prospector. He spent most of his time on the desert and in out-of-the-way places looking for gold. He carried everything he needed in a pack on his donkey. The prospector himself walked. He carried a long stick, wore heavy shoes and had a month's growth of whiskers on his face. He was used to deserts, he said and he had no fears whatever of being alone in the vast desolate country. There had been a heavy blow a night or two earlier, a first rate sandstorm, but he and his donkey found shelter on the safe side of a great rock and waited there till it passed.

"How long did it blow?" Uncle Mario asked.

The prospector took out a match and lit up his pipe.

"Oh, eight or ten hours," he said. "It covered up the wagon tracks, but it wasn't what you'd call a bad blow."

"Covered the trail, hunh?"

"You won't have any trouble, though. You'll see more hills as you get further west. Just make sure you keep them to your right. You can't get lost. If you do, you'll run into Salton Sea after a while, and you can straighten yourself out from that. Mecca will be sort of northwest to you."

"Thanks, friend."

"Good luck, amigos."

Two more days passed. Then suddenly Miguel noticed that Pancho looked bewildered. Riding along at the head of the herd, he seemed uncertain which way to turn.

"Looks like we've come to it."

"Come to what, Uncle Mario?"

"Remember what the old prospector said about the sandstorm?"

Then Miguel looked about and saw for himself. There was no longer a trace of the wagon trail they had followed thus far on the desert. Sand had swept it clean off the earth. Away in the distance, however, a faint, shadowy rim of dove-gray hills could be detected.

"Well, I can see the hills anyhow."

"From now on we'll have to follow our noses."

And that is just what they did. But it was not easy. While they managed to keep the distant hills to their right, often they found themselves plodding through soft sand that put a great burden upon the horses. The animals sweated and puffed. Hours passed and still they seemed to be just as far from those hills as if they had been standing still. Uncle Mario's face looked pinched and worried. Miguel began to feel uneasy.

How terrible it would be to plod along like this with the distant hills in sight and never be able to reach them! Miguel shuddered. The desert was a fascinating but fearful place to be when you came upon hills that were forever far away, so far away. Even the broncos seemed distressed. All of them were showing the strain of the hot journey and the short rations. They looked drawn and thin. They were irritable beasts now, ready to bite and kick at the slightest annoyance.

Hours passed slowly. The sun sank low. Still the hills were far away and the going remained doubtful. Presently the sun reached the horizon and a lovely painted sunset filled the sky.

"Ah," Miguel exclaimed, forgetting his anxiety.

Uncle Mario's face lighted up with a smile. Old Juan's sharp, hard eyes commenced to twinkle. Suddenly Colima began singing "La Golondrina." And while they were all still in this gay mood, a flashing body of water came into sight far to the left. Miguel knew now for sure that they were near Mecca.

"There won't be any stopping now," Uncle Mario said. "We're out of water for the broncos. We'll have to make Mecca if it takes till midnight, but I feel lots better."

"I'm not tired," Miguel assured him. "I could keep going all night so long as I know we're not lost."

Colima heard him and laughed.

"So you thought we were lost, did you? Ha-ha! I bet you were scared a plenty."

"You were too, I bet."

"To tell the truth, I didn't feel so good," Uncle Mario confessed. "I don't blame you, Miguel."

"Well, you were too brave to let on, Miguel," Colima said, calling across the herd. "That shows you're no coward."

This made Miguel feel happy, but he knew now that he had talked too soon when he said he could keep going all night. All of a sudden it seemed, his eyes commenced to feel heavy. My-oh-my, he thought, if I could only shake this sleep out of my eyes.

Once or twice he nodded. Once he nearly fell off his horse and when they finally reached the edge of the place called Mecca, he curled up on the ground and went to sleep before Juan could even get a fire started.

Chapter VIII
The New Colt
∾ତ⌣

Everybody slept late the next morning. The sun
was high when Miguel finally opened his eyes. The herd had
wandered a short distance, but the broncos seemed more
than pleased with their improved fortune. They were ankle
deep in a patch of brownish grass feasting joyously.

Actually the spot looked little better than the rest
of the desert, but Miguel discovered while he still lay
on the ground, that there were important differences.
There were trees—though they were about the dullest,
dreariest, skimpiest trees you'd find anywhere—and a
scattering of little old dwelling shacks in the vicinity.
Best of all, there was water. One shack had a pump in
the yard. Another had a well with an arrangement for
raising and lowering a bucket. A mile or two away there
were palm trees, and beyond that, mountains.

Miguel rose from his sleeping place, stretched his
legs and arms and yawned.

"Ho hum," he said. "Feel like I could stretch
a mile."

Hearing these words, Colima roused
himself slowly.

"What are you talking about, Miguel? Go back
to sleep: It's too early to make noise."

Miguel laughed.

"Late you say? Look at the sun."

"I bet he wake up pronto when I tell the news,"
Old Juan grunted, pouring water from a pail into his
coffee pot. "You bet my life that'll wake him up."

"What's that?" Colima asked, rising on his elbow.

"What's happened?"

Old Juan smiled faintly under his heavy mustache.

"Poco tiempo you find out. Pancho tell you."

"Well, it better be good," Colima warned him. "You make me lose my beauty nap. It better be good news, Old Juan."

"Where's Uncle Mario? Where's Pancho?" he asked.

The old weather-beaten, leather-skinned horseman continued to prepare breakfast. He seemed to be enjoying his little secret, and he plainly did not mean to give it away too soon.

"You see those trees?" he said, pointing with a thumb over his left shoulder. "Well, go there wash your face. You find out."

Colima and Miguel made a race for the clump. Before they reached the little clump Miguel heard his uncle talking and Pancho's voice grunting answers. A moment later, he saw the two men standing near a water trough. There was a pump beside the trough and a puddle on the ground where the water had overflowed. One of the young bronco mares stood in the shade of a small tree. Beside her, on the ground, there was something that Miguel couldn't at first see plainly. When he and Colima drew near, however, they found Pancho and Uncle Mario inspecting a newborn colt. It was a frail, gangling young thing with very long legs, too weak yet to stand of its own strength, but its eyes were bright and it seemed to be more than pleased with the new world it was seeing for the first time.

"A colt!" Miguel exclaimed. "Gee, Colima, what

do you know about that?"

"I had an idea something like that was going to happen," the slender young horseman said, smiling, "but I didn't think it would be this soon."

"Me either," Uncle Mario said, looking up. "How do you like it, Miguel?"

"Grand," Miguel assured him. "But I never saw one so small."

"Yes, he is small all right."

Miguel promptly forgot Old Juan's reminder to wash his face. He was too busy looking at the new colt. The tiny, long-legged thing lay helplessly on the ground near its mother, a happy, surprised look on its face, not knowing just what to think of the wonderful sunshiny earth.

The bronco mare, mother of the new colt, had been given some oats in a box- something special to celebrate the birth of her young one. She stood with her head in the box, eating eagerly, but showing by an occasional glance that she was jealously proud of her new colt.

"Can't he stand up?" Miguel asked.

"Well, yes," Uncle Mario said. "But just a little. His legs are still wobbly."

"Two-three days he be strong—fuerte," Pancho said, drawing up the muscle of his right arm to show what he meant.

The others laughed, knowing that Pancho was exaggerating.

"Just the same, I don't see how he's going to keep up when we get to moving." Colima said.

That was quite a thought. Miguel turned it round and round in his head. Just how were they going to manage with a tiny new colt on their hands. Certainly he couldn't walk all day, even if they were to travel very slowly for his sake. Why, even the full-grown horses became tired after a long day in the hot sun. And this little fellow—oh, he looked so shiny and frail there on the ground—how could he hope to finish the long trip with the herd?

"That's something to think about, Uncle Mario," Miguel said. "We can't leave him here, can we?"

"We could, but we wouldn't," Uncle Mario smiled.

"I'm glad of that. I'll take care of him, Uncle Mario. I've always wanted a colt to take care of and raise up to be a grown horse for my—my own."

"Maybe you could carry him in the saddle with you, Miguel," Colima laughed. "Let him ride bareback behind."

That seemed funny to Pancho, too.

"Never mind about that saddle business," Uncle Mario said. "We'll find a way to look after this young fellow. And he'll be yours, Miguel. You've got your wish."

"We won't sell him in Los Angeles?"

"No, we'll take this one back with us. Angelita will be surprised to see you with a colt of your own."

"I'll say she will. Thanks, Uncle Mario, muchas, muchas, muchas gracias."

"But remember, you'll have to take good care of him all the rest of the way."

"Don't worry, Uncle Mario," Miguel said earnestly. "Never worry about that."

They all took a cool drink at the pump, and then they went away to let the mother and the young one have a little time to themselves. There was a pleasing scent in the air for, by now, Old Juan had breakfast ready. Miguel was almost finished eating when he remembered that he had not washed his face. By that time, it was too late to worry about it.

Chapter IX
Sandstorm

Several days passed before there was any serious talk about leaving the vicinity of Mecca. After the hard days on the desert, the herd seemed so famished it could scarcely get enough to eat.

"Might as well take our time," Uncle Mario said to Miguel one day as the two rode their horses down rows of date palms a short distance from Mecca.

"It'll give the colt more time to get strong."

The uncle smiled, removed his sombrero and dried his forehead with a large colorful handkerchief.

"Yes, that's true," he said, "but what's more important to me, it will give the herd time to put a little flesh on their bones. Maybe you didn't notice, but they've gotten pretty thin on the slim pickings they've been getting during the past few weeks."

"Even here the grass looks dry and parched," Miguel observed.

"But that makes no difference. It's still good food. And the broncos like it. I can see improvement in them."

"Isn't there any more desert ahead, Uncle Mario?"

"Yes, a good bit more. But there are towns scattered along the way. The worst of the trip is behind—unless we run into a blow."

"A sand storm, you mean?"

"That's the greatest danger."

"But what about the colt?"

"Still worried about your colt, hunh? Well, I've been keeping something a secret from you, Miguel, but

I suppose I can tell it now."

"If it's about the colt, Uncle Mario, please don't keep it any longer."

"Well first, what are you going to call the young one?"

Miguel hesitated a moment. Not that he had failed to consider a name for the colt—not by any means—but he was not sure how the name he had in mind would appeal to his uncle. He was a little bit shy about making the suggestions.

"I've thought of two or three names," he said.

"Yes, fine. But which one shall it be?"

"How would Tony be?"

"Excellent. That's the name of your brother."

"Even if he wasn't my brother, I'd like that name."

"You must ask your mother sometime who gave Antonio his name," Uncle Mario said with a proud twinkle in his eye.

"I bet I can guess."

"No, don't guess. Wait and ask your mother. Now about the secret. I have bought a wagon, Miguel. I bought it from the man who lives over there in that white house and owns these date palms."

"So we can give the colt a ride when he gets tired."

"You're a good guesser, but I wonder if you can guess whose job it will be to drive the new wagon."

"Mine, of course."

"Right again."

They reached the camp spot and told the news to the others. All agreed that another wagon would make traveling easier for all concerned as well as providing a lift for the colt at such times as his long, wobbly legs might need rest. But they were even more delighted when Uncle Mario told them that he would wait a few more days before making a fresh start.

Near Mecca, warm breezes sometimes blew in off the desert, but the nights were pleasant. The sky was blue and rich with stars as Miguel lay on his blanket. Several times Miguel thought of his mother and father, his little sister, and his older brother who was seventeen and practically a man. He thought of Maximiliano, the cook's boy. He could close his eyes as he lay on the ground and see the family eating supper with candles on the table. He could see his mother with her jewelry on and a flower in her hair as she sat in the easy chair in the patio watching Señor Del Monte at his painting. He could hear Angelita's voice in the kitchen where she'd gone to entertain and help the cook. But he couldn't see his brother Antonio in Mexico City at the art school, because Miguel had never been there and didn't know what the city looked like.

He missed his family, especially now that he had the colt, and he could hardly wait until he returned and led the young creature into the yard. What a surprise that would be to them. Miguel hoped it would be nearly Christmas then so Antonio would be home from school. He would like to tell his brother his experiences and show him the colt that was Miguel's very own.

A few more days passed, and then came the morning on which Uncle Mario determined to start out again. The herd was very frisky. The broncos looked dusty and wild, but they had some flesh on their bones

now. Nobody could call them skinny. The two wagons
were packed. Uncle Mario was to drive the one that
Old Juan had been driving before, so Old Juan was told
to get in the saddle and help Colima and Pancho keep
the herd together. Miguel took his place in the new
wagon. Behind this wagon, with a rope around her neck,
was tied the bronco mare. She was still a wild horse,
unaccustomed to ropes and halters, but with her young
one in the wagon where she could see it all the time,
she did not rebel against following. So, whistling and
shouting to one another, the horsemen rode out from
the camp spot and in just a few moments had the broncos on the move again. The wagons came along behind.

The day passed without event, and at evening they
rested near a railroad junction. There was a cluster of
wooden buildings and a water tower there, and Pancho
found a spot where there was enough dry, stubby grass
to feed the broncos. They spent the night and the next
morning got an early start on the next leg of the journey. Two days later they were following a twisting road
through cactus country when a small wind commenced
to blow.

It was not much trouble to them when it first
came up. In fact, Miguel thought it felt good after
so many blistering hot days. He also liked the sound
it made as it came off the distant hills with a soft
murmur, and he enjoyed listening to the changed
sound as it gathered speed in the open country and
finally came whistling past the herd and the wagons.

Uncle Mario shook his head and began to look
worried. He took off his hat and let the dry wind blow

through his long black hair, lifting it from his head and whipping it about roughly. Pancho lowered his face and raised a hand to shield his eyes whenever a gust passed him. Colima and Old Juan tied handkerchiefs around their faces like bandits, leaving only enough room to peep out. Still the wind wasn't really bad, not yet. Miguel began to think that if this was what they called a sand storm, he rather liked it.

The herd kept moving as the horsemen urged them on anxiously, but they turned their heads away from the direction of the wind and sometimes even gave the blow their tails in order to keep their eyes away from the sand that was just now beginning to fly. About this time Miguel noticed that the horizon ahead of them was very hazy. The sky had a dark reddish tinge like a curtain of dull fire.

"I'm afraid it's caught us," Uncle Mario called between the gusts.

"A sandstorm?"

The uncle nodded.

"Better tie a bandana around your face — like this. That blowing sand... ." But the wind cut his words short and carried them away. Steadily it blew, and steadily it increased in force, hurling larger and larger quantities of sand before it. The whisper with which at first it rose grew to a roar, but the herd and the horsemen struggled with all their strength to keep moving. The young colt in Miguel's wagon was sheltered by the canvas cover, but the rocking of the wagon and the noisy winds startled him. He opened his eyes very wide.

"Don't mind this," Miguel whispered. "You'll

be all right, Tony. It's noisy, I know, but noise won't hurt you."

Several times Miguel was on the verge of speaking to his uncle, but the wind was so strong it forced the words back down his throat. The sand rose in such dense clouds he couldn't even see Pancho distinctly up there at the head of the broncos. In the western sky the sun turned the color of blood. Still the company kept moving slowly, kept fighting against the storm. Then, all of a sudden, Miguel realized that they had stopped.

Pancho, his horse plowing sand as he walked, came back to the wagons and asked Uncle Mario what they were going to do about it.

"I guess we're not making too much headway," Uncle Mario suggested.

"Headway?" Pancho laughed. "Not much, señor. Still we ought to be able to find a better spot than this."

"Maybe yes. We'll see."

Pancho returned to the lead, and presently the hard pull had begun again. The little burros hitched to the two wagons seemed to stand the strain better than anyone else. They lowered their heads almost to the ground, put more strength into their strides and kept moving ahead with stout determination. Miguel spread a blanket over the young creature in the wagon behind him and drew another around himself. He was not really cold, but somehow a blanket felt good.

Suddenly a small hill rose ahead of them near the road. A moment or two later Colima raised his hand to indicate that there was something in front. Miguel had sand in his eyes and grit in his mouth in spite of his precautions. He chewed down on sand whenever he brought his teeth together; he seemed to have handfuls of sand under his lids. When they came to the slopes of the low hill, however, he drew his wagon close beside Uncle Mario's, rinsed his mouth out with water from a canvas bottle, and blinked till his eyes were more comfortable.

The burros were unhitched. The herd huddled close around the wagons. Finally the storm died down. The wind continued strong. But with the hill to break some of its force, Old Juan got out his rations and started to serve some food, gritty and cold. Miguel didn't enjoy the meal because there was sand in everything, but he ate a little.

That night when Miguel curled up in the bottom of the wagon to sleep, the young colt was so near him he could stretch out his hand and touch his head. He could stroke his side and feel his heart beating. The colt was warm and silky. Outside the wind howled and the sand streamed against the canvas covering of the wagon. Inside it was snug and safe, and Miguel was not afraid. He had his pet near him. There was nothing to worry about. Let the old sandstorm roar if it wanted to! And roar it did — all night long.

Chapter X
Journey's End

Twice that night Miguel woke up briefly. The first time it seemed that something had struck the wagon and almost overturned it. He couldn't see the sky through the opening in the wagon's top. The wind was frightful, but Tony was sleeping well. His mother was eating hay, her head in the back of the wagon. Miguel turned over and went back to sleep. Next time he opened his eyes it was nearly morning. The sky had cleared and the wind had slackened. He could even see a few stars, and, by dawn, all was changed. The wind had died down. The sun came up warm and strong. Miguel rose, uncovered the young colt and climbed out on the ground. To his surprise, he found the sand nearly hub deep around the wheels of the wagons. The broncos all looked drowsy and worn-out. Their heads were low.

"We won't go far today," Uncle Mario said. "The herd's in bad shape."

"They had a hard night," Colima said.

But the burros were hitched and the company moved on for two or three more hours. Then, finding a railroad junction where they could get water and some grass for the animals, they stopped and called it a day.

From there on the journey was easy. Mountains, yes, and steep climbs, but no more deserts and blazing suns. Then they struck the downgrade and Miguel often had to use the brake on his wagon. Orange groves appeared with ripe golden fruit hanging on the trees. There were grape vineyards, miles and miles of them.

Forests of tall eucalyptus trees grew along the roadside. This was California.

Then, three days later, as twilight fell, they reached the big city of Los Angeles and headed directly for the old plaza. It seemed a good bit like his own village to Miguel. The green circle, the watering troughs, the Mexicans sitting nodding on the benches, the horses and carts, the old adobe church across the street — everything seemed familiar and friendly and like home to Miguel. The main differences were the street cars with their clanging bells, the tall buildings off to the south, the elegant carriages driven by well-to-do Americans, and the lights of the city that were now just commencing to wink. There were even a few horseless carriages — automobiles.

"Well, here we are," Uncle Mario said as his wagon came to a stop.

Miguel suddenly felt sleepy. After looking forward to this moment for so many days, he had finally reached the goal, but now he was tired, very tired. His eyes were heavy. He couldn't keep back a long yawn.

"Now what, Uncle Mario?" he said drowsily.

"Sleepy, hunh? Well, I don't blame you. But it's too late to try to find Chona's home tonight. We'll stay here with the herd and tomorrow morning we'll see what we can do about selling the broncos."

"Not this one," Miguel said, stroking the pert ear of the colt.

"No, not that one and not his mother," Uncle Mario agreed.

The horsemen gave all the broncos time to drink

their fill at the watering troughs around the plaza, then led them a short distance away and prepared to pass the night in shifts, one sleeping in Uncle Mario's wagon while two tended the herd. Miguel and his uncle helped Tony, the colt, to the ground. He was strong enough now to stand on his own legs, and Uncle Mario thought it would do him good to frisk about a little.

Next morning when Miguel woke on his pallet on the bed of the wagon, the sale of the broncos was already in progress though dawn was just breaking. The eastern sky was pearly gray, but dozens of men were walking about the plaza. A stone's throw away, where Colima and Pancho and Old Juan had kept the herd, Uncle Mario was busily making deals for one after another of the lively, untamed little horses from Mexico.

Miguel rubbed the remaining sleep from his eyes. Tony, his tail switching, was standing beside his mother, both filled with wonder and excitement. Miguel climbed down from the wagon, washed his face at the water spout and walked over to where the strange men were examining the broncos and leading them away, one by one, with ropes thrown around their necks. From the first words he heard, he learned that Uncle Mario was getting fifteen dollars a piece for the broncos. Not a big price as horses go, but not bad for wild broncos and certainly a good profit as Uncle Mario had calculated.

While the sale went on with more and more men coming and going, everybody except Miguel continued to be busy. With throwing ropes over first one neck then another, with keeping the herd together, the horse-

men had never before had so much to do. And Uncle Mario was trying to answer questions on all sides and dicker with half a dozen men at a time. After Miguel had walked around the plaza and looked and listened till he was tired, he sat on a curbstone to wait for his uncle.

A flock of pigeons came down from the sky and settled on the pavement near him. Miguel went to the wagon and got a handful of grain from a feedbag. This he fed to the pigeons bit by bit. Then he rested his elbows on his knee and tried to think how far he was from home. Oh, it must have been more miles than he could count, but the hard journey was over now. He and Uncle Mario would rest a few days at Aunt Chona's — when they found it — and start back home. Going back would be no trouble. They wouldn't have to herd any animals. What was even better, all of them could ride in the wagons. The trip would be easier this way, and being easier it wouldn't seem long.

By noon Miguel was terribly hungry. More than half of the herd had been disposed of, but there were still many broncos on hand. Uncle Mario came over to the water spout and took a good drink.

"Hungry, Miguel?" he asked in a voice hoarse from so much talking.

The boy's eyes looked sad with longing. He really felt nearly starved but he refused to complain.

"Guess I can wait as long as you can," he said.

"That's the boy! We won't be long now."

"But you still have a hundred or more broncos."

"Listen, Miguel," Uncle Mario whispered. "We're getting good prices for the horses. More than we expected. I have promised one man, who is a dealer, that I'll sell him all I have left at one o'clock for ten dollars a head. That's really all I expected to get for any of them, but it looks now like I'll dispose of two hundred animals for fifteen dollars a piece. All together I'm pleased. We'll have a fine lunch, Miguel, even if we did miss our breakfast."

By one o'clock Uncle Mario had not only disposed of his herd, he had put his other horses and burros in a livery stable to board till he was ready to make the homeward trip. The colt, Tony, and its mother were left there, too. All this done, the four men and the boy entered a restaurant near the plaza and ate the best meal they had enjoyed since they left home, enchiladas, frijoles, and all the things they had on the table in Mexico.

While they were at the table, Uncle Mario gave each of his horsemen some money. They gave him the name of the hotel where they intended to spend their stay in Los Angeles, and he told them he would get in touch with them when he was ready to start out again. Then, the three rose from the table, each one shook hands with their boss, complimented him on their successful trip, and patted Miguel on the back.

"You stood it fine, kid," Colima smiled. "Never cried once either."

They all laughed.

"How about when he fell into the river?" Uncle Mario asked.

"Oh, that doesn't count," Colima assured him. "You'll have lots to tell your mother and father when you get home, Miguel."

"Yes, I will."

Pancho and Old Juan smiled under their heavy mustaches as they rolled cigarettes.

"Someday he make strong guy — like his old man," Pancho said.

"Sure," Old Juan grunted. "Muy toro."

That amused all of them because this is a humorous Mexican expression which means something like "strong as an ox" and it sounded very playful when applied to a small boy like Miguel. Miguel smiled proudly. Everybody laughed. And the group broke up in the best of spirits.

CHAPTER XI
City of the Angels

"Los Angeles," said Uncle Mario. "What a
beautiful name — City of the Angels."

"It is a beautiful city, too," said Miguel, for
certainly it was. There were wide clean streets, enormous
buildings, and speeding cars full of people. Yet there
were palm trees and flowers, too, and parks with foun-
tains in them. And the people were almost all speaking
a language Miguel did not understand — English. But
the people were nice people.

Miguel and his uncle walked down North Main
Street and bought a few fresh new clothes in the little
stores. Later they stopped at the post office and sent
letters and post cards back home. Uncle Mario also
sent a good portion of his money back to his own bank,
explaining to Miguel that he didn't want to be carrying
so much cash in his pockets. There was always the danger
of losing it that way. When this was done, the two went
out and shopped a bit more. Uncle Mario suggested that
they buy presents for Aunt Chona and her two children,
and Miguel thought the idea a good one.

Finally, Uncle Mario rested his bundles on the
sidewalk, took a small notebook from his pocket and
began turning pages.

"Now let me see if I can find that address," he
said. He turned a few more pages then stopped. "Yes,
here it is. We'll have to catch a street car, I know. It's
outside of town."

Half an hour later the two got off an inter-urban
car at the suburb of Watts and walked down a dusty main

street. They made two or three turnings and came to a lane shaded by low trees. This led them to the door of a small cottage behind a hedge with flowering bushes all around the house. Miguel and his uncle swung the gate open, went down the path, and knocked at the door.

A handsome woman came to the door.

"Mario!" she exclaimed. "And this is Miguel!" She threw her arms around one and then the other.

"Chona," her brother said, "It's good to see you."

"You've come a long way."

"Yes," he said. "We've had quite a trip."

"And you, Miguel, how did you like it?"

"Fine," he assured her. "It's been wonderful."

She showed them to a room and made them feel at home. Later that afternoon when they were refreshed and at ease, Aunt Chona's two near-grown children came home. They were dancers. Their names were Carlos and Raquel, and they had been away rehearsing all afternoon. They were delighted to see their uncle and their young cousin. In fact, they were so cheerful and gay that almost immediately Miguel started telling them about the trip, the sandstorm, the plunge in the Colorado River and most important of all, about the colt, Tony.

Carlos and Raquel were as pleased by their presents as was Aunt Chona. They said it was just like Uncle Mario to be so thoughtful. Also, they showed Uncle Mario the stable at the back of their lot and made him promise to bring Tony and the mother from the livery stable the very next day and keep the two there

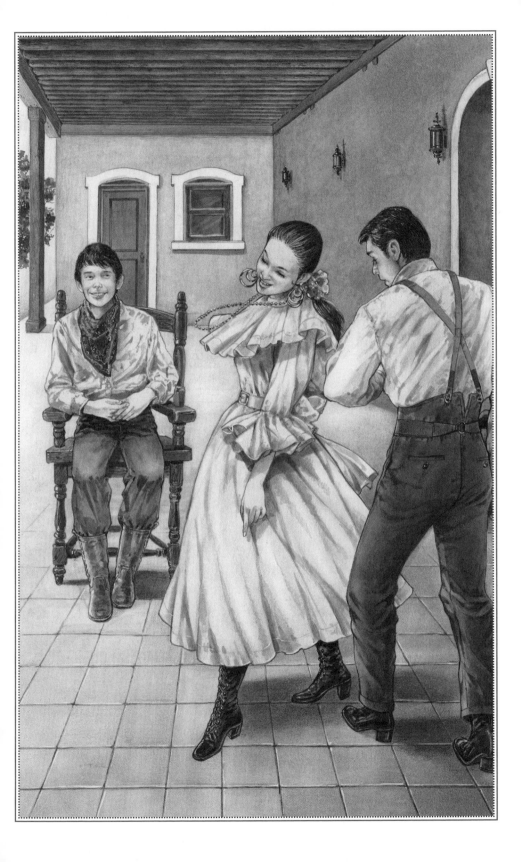

until it was time to leave. This was especially pleasing to Miguel, for he had already begun to wonder how well his colt would fare in that strange place. The next day one of the men from the livery stable brought the mare and the colt out to Watts.

Carlos and Raquel showed Miguel some of the charming dances they were learning. Both of the young dancers were slim, tall and beautiful in motion. Both of them had lustrous black hair.

Miguel told them how his own brother, who was as old as Carlos, was studying art in Mexico City and hoping to be an artist like Señor Del Monte.

"How wonderful," Raquel said. "But what are you going to be, Miguel?"

The boy didn't know what to answer. He had never made up his mind definitely just what career he would follow when he grew up. Besides, his beautiful tall cousin was so sweet and kind that he began to think the most important thing might be to please her.

"Would you mind if I learned to dance, too?" he asked shyly.

"Not at all, Miguel," she laughed. "But make sure it's the thing you like best of all."

Miguel was not sure he liked dancing best of all. In fact, he doubted it, but he was glad Raquel seemed pleased. He also felt that she would not mind if he settled on something else, so he didn't feel bound to follow in her footsteps and the footsteps of Carlos.

During the days that followed Aunt Chona and her children took Miguel and Uncle Mario for long rides in a rubber-tired surrey with a white top. They drove to the harbor down an unpaved road that ran through a eucalyptus grove and came out near a slough. When they were still miles away, the smell of the sea reached them. They spread their lunch on a cliff looking down on the water. On another day they drove through miles of orange groves to the mountains. There was always something to do, some place to go. The time passed swiftly.

Two and then three weeks passed. Tony, who received constant attention from the household, grew remarkably fast. He also learned to beg for sugar. Then one day when the folks were all sitting on the veranda, he got over the fence and gave Carlos and Miguel and Uncle Mario a fine chase through the streets of Watts before they got him back in again.

"That's the limit!" Uncle Mario said afterwards. "We'd better start thinking about home, Miguel."

Aunt Chona and her children tried to prevail upon him to stay longer, but Uncle Mario told them he had already stayed a week longer than he had planned. They hoped to be home for Christmas. As much as he and Miguel had enjoyed their visit in Aunt Chona's home, they must remember that Miguel had never been away from home for such a long time and that his mother might get worried. So it was decided. Next week they would leave.

Once more Miguel and his uncle went shopping for presents. They bought something for every member of the family at home. Then one evening the wagons were loaded and the burros staked in a field for the night. Next morning before daylight Miguel and his uncle rose and dressed. Aunt Chona and Carlos and Raquel got up early and had a farewell breakfast with them. While they were still at the table, there was a knock at the door. Colima, Pancho and Old Juan, the horsemen had arrived. Uncle Mario showed them where the animals were staked and asked them to hitch the burros to the wagons while he and Miguel finished their meal. A few moments later they were all on the veranda saying goodbye. Then the two wagons pulled away.

Miguel looked back and saw his aunt waving a handkerchief. Carlos was standing at her side. Raquel, who had followed them to the gate, was beside the hedge. She was as beautiful as a dream. Miguel thought he would try to tell Antonio what a lovely cousin they had. Maybe his big brother would paint her picture sometime.

The wagons rocked along steadily on the dusty roads. In a little while the tardy sun came up. They were headed home.

CHAPTER XII

And Back Again
❧

Once more they crossed the desert, but it was
different now. Without the herd of broncos it was easy
to carry enough water to last them from one well to
the next. There were no more sandstorms either, and
fresh wagon tracks over the sandy country made it easy
to follow the trail. Miguel realized suddenly that the
next day they would be crossing the swift Colorado River
again soon. A week later they would be home, perhaps.

Young Tony was getting stronger and friskier by
the hour. He could now run along all day, following
his mother and scampering around the wagons. Miguel
got out sometimes and walked beside the colt. It gave
the boy's legs exercise and seemed to rest them from
the discomfort of sitting in the wagon so long at a time.
Everyday, it seemed to Miguel, the colt learned to know
him a little better.

"Come back here, Tony," Miguel would call,
slapping his hands together to draw the colt's attention.
"Mind where you're going. If you run into some of
that cactus, you won't forget it soon — the way it will
stick you."

The young creature always stopped in time.
Whether he understood Miguel's warning or whether
he knew already the dangers of prickly cactus clumps was
hard to tell, but he always stopped in time. Once Miguel
had to shout at him very loudly for another reason.

"Look out!" the boy cried, "Look out!"

Tony hesitated, looked down innocently, and
there, almost under one of his hoofs, was a rattlesnake

curled up ready to strike.

"What's wrong, Miguel?" asked Uncle Mario who had until this moment been nodding on a wagon seat. At the same moment, Colima jumped to the ground. He was a trifle late, however, as Miguel had already planted a stone squarely on the neck of the rattler.

"Well, guess that takes care of him," Colima said. "You didn't waste any time, Miguel."

"No, he was about to strike," the boy said. "I heard his rattlers."

"Lucky for Tony you were on the job. Snake bites are not good for a young colt."

After that incident things went well. Tony had learned his lesson. He didn't get near any more snakes.

Finally the wagons reached the river, and Larry came across with his father to ferry the company through the swift current.

"Say, what's that you got, Miguel?" the boy cried out, seeing the young colt.

"He's mine," Miguel said proudly. "Born at Mecca. Uncle Mario gave him to me."

Uncle Mario and his horsemen talked with the ferryman about their trip, their hardships, and their final success in disposing of their herd in Los Angeles. As they talked, they drove the first wagon onto the odd, flat-bottomed ferry and rode across with it. Miguel and Larry stayed behind with the other wagon. Tony also lingered behind, frightened by the swift water and remaining near his mother.

"What happened on the trip?" Larry asked.

Miguel told him about the gypsy boy who had

broken his bow and he was tempted to tell Larry the result of the fight in which he and the bigger boy engaged, but he hesitated for fear it would sound like boasting. Instead, Miguel gave a description of the sandstorm. Then he told what he had seen in Los Angeles, that very big city. He talked about his Aunt Chona, Carlos, and especially Raquel, his tall pretty cousin who danced on the stage with her brother. Finally, he told about the rattler that had threatened Tony just the day before.

"Boy, you've had a trip, a real one!" Larry exclaimed.

The ferry returned and took the saddle horses. A few moments later it came again and took the second wagon along with Larry and Miguel and Tony. On the east bank of the stream goodbyes were said, and the company continued its homeward journey through the sunlight.

The days passed slowly now, for Miguel's mind was set on home, and that made the way seem long. He was thinking about Christmas, too, for it was December.

"How many more days?" he asked his uncle one afternoon.

"Christmas? Oh, that's five days yet."

"Seems like a long time," Miguel complained.

"Long? Why, these are the shortest days of the year."

They grew silent again. Slowly, steadily the wagons rolled along across Arizona. The sky was bright, but the weather was not so warm as it had been on the earlier trip. A nip of winter was in the air, especially at night and in the morning. Miguel slept wrapped in blankets, and when he woke up, he could see his breath like smoke. But all day long, hour after hour, the burro teams plodded along, the wagons rolled, and eventually they crossed the border again and turned directly toward the south.

"Think we'll have any trouble with bandits?" Miguel asked.

The horsemen laughed with Uncle Mario and blew puffs of cigarette smoke into the air.

"Not likely," his uncle said. "What do they want with us now? The herd's gone."

"Maybe money," Old Juan suggested without seeming to be very much worried.

"Tell him about the money, Miguel," Uncle Mario chuckled.

"Uncle Mario sent it home to the bank," Miguel explained. "He sent it at the post office that first day in Los Angeles."

"Good." Old Juan grunted.

Miguel didn't ask about the saddle horses they were leading, but he imagined they might be attractive to bandits. He thought about them at night. Most especially he thought about Tony. He wondered if any bandit could be mean enough to take such a small colt from its mother or the boy who owned it. When he thought of this, he always woke up and looked around to make sure that Tony was near and that no danger was lurking under the stars.

The first night, nothing happened. The second night was the same. But at sunrise following the third night, after they had crossed the border into Mexico, Miguel woke up to find the bronco mare and her colt were nowhere to be seen.

"They're gone," he cried, waking the men with his outburst. "They're gone, both of them. Oh, where's Tony?"

The men tumbled out of the wagons in great excitement. Sure enough, there was no bronco mare in sight! No Tony!

Miguel knew he would not be able to keep back the tears for long, so he rushed off toward the scrubby trees a short distance away. He didn't want to be seen crying now — after making a reputation for never once having cried on the journey west. But before he reached the shelter of the trees, his face was wet with tears. He kept walking, trying to get a safe distance away. It would be terrible to have the men come upon him while he was crying. A few moments later he turned and saw through the leaves that Uncle Mario and the others were throwing saddles across the backs of their horses.

That gave the boy an idea. How much better it would be to saddle up a horse and make a search for his colt than to creep away and cry like a baby. Even if his heart did feel as if it would break, it would be better to try to find Tony. Miguel dried his eyes on his sleeve and hurried back to the wagons.

"Well, I thought you'd want to help us find them," Uncle Mario said. "Colima will help you with that saddle there."

A moment later they were combing the sur-rounding country, riding up embankments, thrashing

through thickets, at dawn, looking on every side for
the little mare and her frisky colt. But the longer they
looked, the less they found. Then when the sun was high
overhead, they turned sadly and started back toward
the wagons. Miguel felt so miserable he couldn't talk,
couldn't say a single word.

When they came within sight of the wagons,
however, he saw something that made his eyes pop open.
Could he believe his eyes? He rode ahead, hurrying with
excitement. Yes, sure enough, there they were, the little
mare and her long-legged colt standing near the burros
and acting for all the world as if nothing had happened.
Where had they been?

"Can you beat this?" Uncle Mario said, greatly
outdone.

One by one the men slid off their saddles. Old
Juan set about to prepare a meal.

"Wild goose chase — that's what I call it," Colima
said.

Miguel was so happy he had no words.

"We could have been home by now," Uncle
Mario said. "This is our last day, you know. Now it will
be night when we arrive."

Their stomachs filled with food and their hearts
unburdened, the company set out once more. They
were among the hills now, and sometimes they were
laboring up a mountainside, sometimes going down.
It was hard on the teams. When night fell, a small
mountain town came into view. Tiny lights could be
seen. Miguel knew that town. It was his home.

Their wagons reached the gate of Miguel's house

after another hour of driving. There were candles burning inside the house. Someone was in the patio. Miguel ran to the little gate and called. When Maximiliano let the boy in, Tony entered, too.

"What's this?" the yardboy asked.

"Oh, you'll find out, Maximiliano. He's mine. I'll tell you everything later. It may take a month. Where's my mother and everybody?"

Uncle Mario reached the patio as the inner door was being opened for Miguel just in time to see the tumultuous greeting the boy was receiving from his family. And there, standing among the others, was Antonio, home for Christmas! Uncle Mario called to his men to drive the wagons into the field where they had kept the herd on the previous stop. Tony danced on the stones of the patio looking amused but puzzled, his hooves twinkling.

A little later, Miguel brought the whole family out to show them his colt. When they had each patted his nose and admired the young creature, they found seats in the patio under the stars and began to pour questions upon Miguel and Uncle Mario.

"Oh, Miguel will have to tell you all about everything," Uncle Mario said, raising his hand to quiet them. We had a fine trip."

Miguel agreed heartily.

Then the two travelers opened their presents and Miguel distributed them — beads for his mother, a bracelet for Angelita, a new pipe for his father, a different kind of pipe for Antonio. Tall candles for the Virgin's shrine. There were some other things for

Maximiliano and his mother.

"Any close calls?" Señor Del Monte asked.

Miguel nodded.

"A rattlesnake almost bit Tony," he said.

"Miguel is too modest to tell you who killed the rattler just as he was about to strike," Uncle Mario said, "but I will. It was Miguel himself."

This seemed to please them all, especially Antonio.

"Good," the older boy said, "I knew you wouldn't be afraid. But what was the prettiest thing you saw, Miguel?"

Miguel didn't have to think long.

"Our cousin, Raquel," he said promptly. "You should see her, Antonio! You would paint her picture if you saw her."

"I hope you've got a good eye," Antonio laughed. "Maybe I will see her someday and I don't want to be fooled."

Antonio and Señor Del Monte lit up their new pipes. The stars grew brighter and brighter over the patio. Miguel sat on a stool beside his mother's chair. Presently he felt her fingers running through his hair. It was good to be home, even when you'd had a fine trip. Angelita turned the new bracelet round and round on her little wrist. It was hard to talk when there was so much to be said. Maximiliano's mother made a steaming kettle of hot chocolate and served them all big mugs full as they sat in the patio. Uncle Mario stretched his legs and leaned back in his chair. Miguel leaned back, too. He looked tired, but happy — happy to be home again.

Afterword

Arna Bontemps and Langston Hughes met in 1924 in Harlem when both men were budding writers in the Harlem Renaissance. They subsequently became good friends and decided to write children's books together. Hughes and Bontemps thought that children, unaffected by the prejudices and biases of adults, could more readily appreciate stories about different people and cultures. The two men wrote stories that invited children to think and dream beyond their own day-to-day worlds.

Mexico was a natural choice for the setting of a children's book; both Bontemps and Hughes had ties to Mexico. Bontemps had Mexican-American neighbors in California during his youth, taught high school Spanish and had in-laws with a ranch in Mexico. Hughes' enchantment with Mexico sprang from his trips there in the 1920s to visit his father, James Hughes, a businessman who resided in Toluca, Mexico.

In a letter dated 21 September 1939, Hughes advised Bontemps to begin a draft of a children's book that includes "something heroic once to keep the faith with the possibilities of the human race and buoy up the Mexicans." Between 1939 and 1941, Bontemps and

Hughes drew on their experiences and research to write *Boy of the Border,* an adventure story that takes place during the turbulent period of the Mexican Revolution that began in 1910. Bontemps asked Hughes to add all of the details about Mexican food and customs based on the latter's experiences living in Mexico. James Hughes' house was the model for the Del Monte hacienda; Maximiliano, the yard boy at the Del Monte house, was patterned after the real Maximiliano who worked at the Toluca home. In 1941, Hughes, to put the finishing touches to the manuscript, took a bus trip across the Arizona desert to ensure that the plants, animals and conditions of the desert were accurately described in the book. Bontemps described the horse sale scene based on his boyhood memories of accompanying his uncle to a sale of wild horses in the Los Angeles plaza. The details about herding horses across a long stretch of desert were provided by Hughes' acquaintance, Garth Jeffers, a former horse herder in New Mexico.

Bontemps and Hughes were convinced that *Boy of the Border* was a great story, possibly eligible for a movie deal and for the Newbery Award presented annually by the American Library Association to the author of the Outstanding American Children's Book. *Boy of the Border,* however, was not published. Lamenting that fact in a 29 August 1955 letter to Hughes, Bontemps noted "... I can't imagine why it was not published. Perhaps the Depression was to blame."

Beginning in the summer of 1955, Bontemps and Hughes revised the manuscript in an attempt to interest a publisher. In what their letters suggest was a strategy to attract publishers, Hughes and Bontemps agreed to let the children's magazine *Jack and Jill* publish a condensed, 10-page version of the book, which was entitled "Broncos Over the Border." The novella appeared in the July, 1956 issue of *Jack and Jill*. The full manuscript of *Boy of the Border*, however, was never published.

❧

    Boy of the Border has now come to life as the book that accomplishes the authors' goal of creating an adventurous and inspiring educational story for young people. The underlying messages of *Boy of the Border* are timely for a world in which all children, and especially children of color, must resist the negative images and be encouraged to believe in themselves as loveable, good, capable and creative. The story presents positive pictures of people whose media images are often demeaning, derogatory and hostile.

    It is another example of the fine literature that Arna Bontemps and Langston Hughes produced for the reading enjoyment of children.

    In preparing *Boy of the Border* for publication, Sweet Earth Flying Press did silent editing, correcting obvious typos and grammatical errors, and ensuring consistency in spelling and word usage. The publisher retained words and expressions in the manuscript that seem outdated, but were commonly used in the 1930s and 1940s when the novel was written.

FIC   Bontemps, Arna
BONTEMPS   Wendell, 1902-1973.

           Boy of the border.

$17.95   Grades 4-6

DATE			

AUG   2010